The Winter Drey

The Winter Drey

THE TRILOGY OF THE TREE
PART II

SEAN DIXON

KEY PORTER BOOKS

Copyright © 2009 Sean Dixon

All rights reserved. No part of this work covered by the copyrights hereon may be reproduced or used in any form or by any means—graphic, electronic or mechanical, including photo-copying, recording, taping or information storage and retrieval systems—without the prior written permission of the publisher, or, in case of photocopying or other reprographic copy-ing, a licence from Access Copyright, the Canadian Copyright Licensing Agency, One Yonge Street, Suite 1900, Toronto, Ontario, M6B 3A9.

Library and Archives Canada Cataloguing in Publication

Dixon, Sean
    The winter drey / Sean Dixon.

(The trilogy of the tree ; pt. 2)
ISBN 978-1-55470-190-2

    1. Vikings—Juvenile fiction. I. Title. II. Series.
PS8557.I97 W55 2009   jC813'.54   C2009-901388-6

The publisher gratefully acknowledges the support of the Canada Council for the Arts and the Ontario Arts Council for its publishing program. We acknowledge the support of the Government of Ontario through the Ontario Media Development Corporation's Ontario Book Initiative.

We acknowledge the financial support of the Government of Canada through the Book Publishing Industry Development Program (BPIDP) for our publishing activities.

Key Porter Books Limited
Six Adelaide Street East, Tenth Floor
Toronto, Ontario
Canada M5C 1H6

www.keyporter.com

Illustrations: Brian Deines
Text design and electronic formatting: Martin Gould

Printed and bound in Canada

09 10 11 12 13 5 4 3 2 1

This book is dedicated to the memory of the maple tree at the end of Columbus Street, a great perch for peregrines.

And also to the memory of Ludmila Cizkova, who was among the first to read *The Feathered Cloak*.

The force that through the green fuse
drives the flower
Drives my green age.
—Dylan Thomas

THIS ISN'T THE BEGINNING of my story. You may already know there's a whole other book that precedes this one. I don't know about you, but I hate it when I'm three chapters into something, not knowing what's going on, only to discover that it's Book Five of a series I've never heard of and is now out of print.

My first book is known as *The Feathered Cloak*. It's old now, by your standards. You might be able to find it in the library. I stopped writing for many years after depicting the death of Morton in that book, because my heart broke, with Freya's, all over again. I apologize for my tardiness and my excessive sensitivity. Still, the whole story happened so long ago that I should be able to pull myself together. And it shouldn't make a difference whether I do my writing tonight or tomorrow or next week or a hundred years from now. I will always remember it as if it were yesterday.

This evening I've lit a new candle, and I'm going back to tenth-century Norway, where a lot more happened than you might find in your history books. My story picks up not long after the last one left off, during the hours after sunset, in a small house with a red-painted door, standing all alone by a field and a forest, where dwells Freya the Bold, hands-down heroine of the first book.

And her little brother, Rolf, hero of the second.

But how can I tell a whole story about Rolf? You might complain that he's just a little boy, even if he's also a giant. He's so shy, you might say. He's gullible. He's naive. He's a big, clumsy oaf. And worst of all, he never speaks more than a single word at a time. Often a single syllable. How can a gullible, clumsy, single-syllable-speaker be at the centre of a story?

Well, he can. That's all I can tell you for now. He can.

1

A Sister Gone

ROLF LAY IN HIS BED, half on top of it, half off of it. He'd removed the legs from the foot of the bed, tilting it lengthwise down to the floor, so that with all his size he could make himself fit. He lay there but could not sleep. The events of the day hovered over him. Just a few hours before, he had taken a pole with a feathered banner and strode through the ranks of Viking soldiers, brandishing it like a spear. Where had he found that kind of courage? And where had that courage gone? Would it come back? Deep down he could feel there had been no great change in him. Not like his sister. His beloved sister. Who could hurl herself up into the sky, slowly, and come back down again, winged.

His sister was winged. Rolf was big and oafish. Freya was winged.

11

Even after all the gains of the day, Rolf still wished he could be less like himself and more like Freya. Because now there was somewhere that Freya could go where Rolf could not follow. Who wouldn't want to go up into the sky? Above the clouds that had covered the land for so long that Rolf could barely remember the way it was before? Just as their mother had left, so too Freya would go and when that time came, Rolf would be by himself. Like when Freya used to wander the woods alone, before they caught the falcon named Morton.

Only this time it would be forever.

"Go on to bed now, Rolf. I'm going to have a talk with your sister."

That's what his father had said. And Rolf, his finger pressed to his own chest, had asked, "Me?"

Meaning, What about me? Will you tell me too? Will you impart to me the lore you're passing on to her?

"I will, Rolf, one day. When you're a little older."

Father and daughter had retreated to the back stoop, where they sat huddled around a candle and spoke in hushed tones. From the kitchen, Rolf could see their breath form a cloud around them as they spoke in the cold air, but the tips of Freya's wings hovered around their bent heads so that he could not make out what they were saying. And so he felt left out. He even began to wonder whether she was being told how he was to blame; how he was the culprit that had driven their mother away. Simply by being born. This was how he remembered it. Too big, he'd been. Too brutish.

Too young.

But Rolf had fought a war today. How could he be too young for anything?

Just three days ago, you could have said he was too young. But then Rolf and Freya—or just Freya, really, with Rolf tagging along—had captured a falcon. A falcon named Morton. And that had changed everything because Morton was an outlaw, on the run from the king. Which meant that suddenly Freya was an outlaw, which meant Rolf was an outlaw too. Together, the three of them had come, in a very short time, to change the history of Norway. There was a new king tonight, a good king, because of their courage. And then Freya did something miraculous that Rolf would never have believed if he had not seen it with his own eyes. Rolf did something miraculous too, but what he had done, in the grand scheme of things, was not quite as miraculous as what his sister had done. He had just been brave. Maybe that wasn't so miraculous. It was certainly not enough to usher him onto the stoop for the lore even now being imparted to his sister by their father.

Rolf struggled not to feel jealous of his sister. After all, he thought, Morton died. And Freya was Morton's friend. So she must be sad. But, then again, she flew. She flew up in the sky, with Morton's wings that became her own. So she must be happy. She must be both happy and sad. She must be confused. It must be very confusing to be Freya right now.

Rolf was trying to explain things to himself so he would stop feeling left out, overlooked, jealous. What else could he do? Maybe this miracle had changed her so much that she would remain forever divided from her own loving little brother. And so he wondered: Would he ever change too? Would he make a friend too? Would he become something great too? If so, could it just hurry up and happen, already? Please?

What else was a lonely boy to do, faced with such questions, but lie in the dark and brood?

He lay in the dark. He brooded.

From the beams above, he heard a rustling. Then a small voice whispering:

"Me," said the voice. "I am going to make history. Not just remember it. Not just write it down and chew it up and make a pillow. No, I'm going to *make* history, as easily as my fellows make a nest. No, I correct myself: I am going to *change* the *course* of history."

There was a squirrel nest up in the rafters. Made of moss, winter straw and bits of everything. Just a month before, a mother squirrel had given birth to a litter. Rolf had heard her chittering to them above the beams just before the sun went down and they all settled in for the night. Followed by the rustling of many small bodies in a small space. Rolf would lie half off his bed and imagine the comfort that came from having several tiny siblings of equal shape and size, all tucked together in a crevice.

But in recent days, there had been much jostling as the young squirrels had left the nest, one by one, to go find nooks of their own. Finally the mother had left too. How she must have worried for her children, striking out on their own into a world with no spring or summer. Rolf heard her heave a final, tiny sigh, resigned, as she made her way. And then everything was quiet and lonesome again, here in his little room. The squirrels were gone.

But they weren't all gone. One squirrel had remained. The one who was up there whispering. Had he, like Rolf, been abandoned by his mother?

"I can see you," said the squirrel finally, allaying all doubt that he was really there. "You're a giant, aren't you? You are. All I have to do is peek over the edge of the rafter and I can see you down there. Too big for this room, you are. Too big for this part of the world, I'll venture. Just like me."

Up in the darkness, Rolf could make out the tiniest glint of an eye. How could this tiny creature claim he was too big for the world? It was a wonder.

"You think I'm too young," said the squirrel. "But aren't you also too young? Isn't this something we have in common? Is this not why we should go together?"

Go together where?

"You can trust me," said the squirrel. "My family goes way back in these parts. So does yours. Way back. And you and I have lived here under the same roof for a very long time."

"No," said Rolf, who had heard the day this squirrel was born.

And then he realized he had spoken out loud. Now they were having a *conversation*.

"Quibble quibble," said the squirrel, who seemed unsurprised, as if they'd been talking the whole time. "So I don't know short and long. If my days have been short, I've got nothing to compare them to. I think they're long. There's nothing longer than a day. Except maybe a night. I've heard tell of longer times, like weeks and months and years. But I don't believe in them. The days and nights I've had so far have given me time enough to learn everything there is to know."

"I doubt that," thought Rolf.

"It's true," the squirrel continued, as if in answer. "Thanks to my mama, who was wise in all things. She taught us everything. We use a dialect called Chkkt, for short, which uses very small words that take no time at all to say. You can tell someone a lot of things very fast. Squirrels, in case you didn't already know, are the world's most scholarly creatures."

"Hmmph," said Rolf, who did not already know.

"But our circumstances prevent us from ever writing anything down. Any squirrel who has ever bothered to write a book has always ended up tearing it up into strips to make his nest warmer and drier. Priorities, priorities. So instead we have developed our memories, right from the beginning, when we're given twenty-syllable names."

"Twenty?" asked Rolf, amazed.

So the squirrel told Rolf his name.

"But you can call me Rat-A-Task for short," he added.

Rolf told the squirrel his name in return. But Rat-A-Task didn't give any sign that he had heard. He was too busy warming to his topic.

"Squirrels," he said, "used to rule the world. Did you know that? My mother told me. Well, no, that's an exaggeration, she didn't tell me that, exactly. She told me that a long time ago there used to be one very important squirrel, who filled a very important position. And she told me that for a long time now, that very important position has not been filled. But she also told me that the time is coming again very soon when there will be an opening, and when that time comes, I intend to fill it!"

Rolf really had no idea at all what this little squirrel was chattering on about. "What?" he asked, meaning what was the position.

"If you come with me," said the squirrel, "I can show you. I could tell you—I have strong descriptive powers—but I would prefer to show you. And if you come with me, I will see that you are rewarded."

"King?" asked Rolf. Meaning: Was it to the king.

"No, not the king!" protested the squirrel. "I will serve a far higher authority than some useless king!"

This was something to think about. The squirrel didn't even care about the king. What's more, he was aware of higher authorities than kings, out there in the big world. He seemed to be an awfully wise squirrel. If Freya had had a wise animal friend, then maybe Rolf could have a wise animal friend too. And this wise animal friend wanted him to go somewhere. That much was clear. Rolf wasn't sure he wanted to go, but . . .

"Where?" he found himself asking.

"I don't have time to tell you now," said Rat-A-Task. "I'll tell you as we go."

He was in a hurry, this squirrel.

"Freya?" asked Rolf, because this squirrel wanted them to leave now, in the middle of the night, and Rolf was very much afraid of the dark. The more, in short, the merrier.

"No, my boy. It's not your sister I've met this fine evening. It's you. And anyway, I've no use for your sister. It's a giant I need."

And then, sounding as if he was counting on his fingers, the squirrel listed the assets of a giant: "One, a giant walks fast. Two, with me on his shoulder a giant walks in the right direction. Three, a giant makes a spectacularly effective bodyguard for a squirrel, though it's true that might be overdoing it a little. And four, what's more, a giant is good at finding other giants."

He concluded, "You might think a young girl with borrowed falcon wings is impressive, but can she do all these things? I don't think so!"

Rolf did not quite understand what the squirrel was talking about. What was a bodyguard? What did it mean to find other giants? Despite these questions, he could not help but be cheered by the list of virtues he possessed that his sister did not. He even laughed a little, quietly, like this: "Heh heh heh."

And then he blushed and clammed up, not wanting to belittle Freya.

Rat-A-Task came skittering down out of the shadows above to perch, bushy-tailed and jumpy, right by the boy's chin.

"And, of course," he said, with a twitch of his nose and a glint in his eye, "it's better for you to leave. Your sister is going to fly out of here tonight, and you'll never see her again. She's not even going to say goodbye. Wouldn't you rather be gone before that happens? After all, there are worse things to be afraid of than the dark."

And so, a single giant shadow lumbers through the night, making a single pair of footprints as it goes. Rolf is wearing a woollen hat, pulled down over his ears. It's true, he is afraid of the dark, but the squirrel's words about his sister have scared him even more. Freya is going to go before the morning, he said. She will not say goodbye, he said. She will probably not even know he's gone ahead of her. Rolf tries not to think about that. How she is going to abandon him.

It does not occur to him how he might be abandoning her.

Earlier, as they entered the woods, Rolf even thought he saw a pair of riders back in the trees just beyond the clearing; saw, hovering just above their heads, the shadow shape of wings.

"There they are," he thought, bitterly, "waiting for my sister."

And so he picked up his pace as he headed into the darkness.

It is perhaps important to mention that Rolf has grown up in a world that does not know what to believe anymore. In his country of Norway, circa 934, there is now a Christian king, even though none of the people he rules are Christians. It makes for confusing times, because the people are not sure they believe in the old Viking gods anymore either. Rolf is like that too. He's just like everyone else in Norway, circa 934, even if he looks a little different. He's just as confused as everyone else. He doesn't know what to believe anymore either.

Except tonight. Tonight, Rolf is going to believe in a little squirrel perched on his shoulder, pointing the way into the unknown. How exciting it is to make such a decision.

But it is perhaps also important to mention that sometimes it can be rash to make a friend so quickly. And perhaps, one day soon, Rolf will be surprised to find that this little squirrel is not like Morton the noble falcon at all.

2

The Sons of Erik Blood-Axe

YOU MIGHT THINK that Rolf the Ranger and Rat-A-Task the Squirrel were the only creatures awake and wandering in the middle of this wintry night, but you'd be wrong. Because Erik Blood-Axe was out there too, standing at the edge of the ocean, watching the black waves tug at the shore.

Erik was too tired and sad to feel the anger that had once set his teeth on edge and brought steam whistling out of his ears. Tonight, he was going to leave behind the land he loved.

With him were his sons, seven boys named Harald who had spent the last month pillaging in Denmark and had missed all the events depicted in the first book, most notably the battle on the Field of Snorre. These sons joined up with their father just after the battle was decided and Norway had been lost to the new Christian king.

Actually, it's not entirely accurate to say they were sons. In fact, two of them were daughters, but it just so happened that the daughters dressed like the sons and wore helmets and did not speak but instead stood guard. All of them—sons and daughters—behaved like boys and called themselves boys, and called themselves Harald, after their grandfather, Harald Finehair, uniter of Norway. A witch had once predicted that the children of Erik Blood-Axe would all be slaughtered except for the one named Harald, who would himself become king. So, naturally, the brothers and sisters had agreed to defy their fate by pricking their fingers and renaming themselves Harald, every single one. You might think this was foolish, but it seems to me if you're going to get snared by a witch's trickery, you should try and get out of it as best you can.

The sons and daughters of Erik Blood-Axe were not normally as confused as the rest of the people of Norway circa 934. Normally, they were bursting with conviction and knew exactly what to believe and what not to believe. Like their father, they rejected the rule of the new Christian king, having always embraced the old Viking ways of their ancestors and cultivated their belief in Odin and the old gods, just in the manner they felt a first family properly should.

At the moment, however, standing with their father at the edge of the sea, the sons and daughters of Erik

Blood-Axe were very confused indeed. Their father, you see, was about to abandon his homeland, and this is something that a Viking king should never do. And so the sons and daughters demanded an explanation.

"You have told us," said Harald the eldest, generously including his brothers and sisters, "that the Viking gods have not revealed themselves to men for many generations. Your father was told by his father who was told by his father, and it goes back like that."

"For ten generations," said Erik. "Yes. Before that, they were here."

"And now they are here again!" shouted Harald, for whom there was nothing more precious than evidence of the old gods.

"But not for us," said Erik. "Not for me."

"You said there were Valkyries on the Field of Snorre," said the son. "Women warriors. Winged. Choosers of the slain!"

"Perhaps," said Erik, who was looking older by the minute. "Perhaps I saw no such thing."

"You promised me," said the boy, almost weeping, his brothers and sisters gathered around him, "that the gods would come back one day. That they would find some way to return and rebuild. You told me, when I was younger."

"You still are young," said Erik. "And I believed it myself when I was young. Eventually, I grew up and saw the world the way it truly was."

"And how is the world truly?"

Erik shrugged. "To put it simply, the world is changing."

"What was it you saw then, tonight, on the battlefield? Did you not say you saw a winged girl? Did you not say her name was Freya? Did she not have Valkyries for servants? Tonight, you witnessed the return of Freya the goddess after ten generations. Who's to say her fellow gods and goddesses are not far behind? And yet you choose to run away!"

"I don't think that's what I saw," said Erik.

"Then what did you see?"

Erik was about to answer, but then he paused. He looked back with his mind's eye. Saw again the image of the girl standing in front of him. Wings sprung from her shoulders. Saw her point to his Christian brother instead of to him.

"I saw someone choose to be the servant of the new Christian God," he said. "If she herself was a god, then I don't understand the gods anymore at all."

"But you said she was a child!" shouted Harald. "Maybe she chose wrong because she's too young and doesn't know how to choose! Maybe she needs to be taught! Maybe . . ." And here the son reached up and put his hands on his father's shoulders and looked into his eyes, pleading for him to understand. "Maybe even now she is searching all over for you again, on that battlefield and beyond, shouting, 'Where are you! I remember now! I remember! Please come back!'"

"Maybe," said Erik. And he smiled at his son's

conviction and shook himself from his grip, raising his finger to test the readiness of the wind.

"You're a Viking," the son went on. "A Norseman! It is a Norseman's duty to honour the gods. Otherwise you're not a Norseman at all! You're just some kind of *Norwegian*!"

"Not even a Norwegian," said Erik. "Since I'm leaving Norway tonight."

"The gods are here," said the eldest, scoffing. "Our young gods are returning to dwell in the clouds and mountains and hills of Norway! They are here. And they will look out from their hiding places and see a Christian King ruling over the land. They will weep with rage and shame."

"They will have to come to Scotland then, if they want to see Vikings," shrugged the former tyrant with a smile. "My son, my son. All the fight has gone from me. Can you not see it? If you wish to stay and fight and die during these dying days of Viking ways, then I will not try to stop you. If you seek to kill some Christians, I will even give you my sword."

And here he drew his blade from its scabbard and offered the handshaft to his son.

"A drawn sword should draw blood," said the eldest, blushing.

"Not when it is a gift from a father to a son," said Erik, simply. "Perhaps one day you will understand that sometimes what looks like a weapon is really a gift."

And so the son, shamed by this admonishment,

took hold of the sword. But he did not say thank you. Because, in truth, he wished for his father himself to stay in Norway, instead of his sword.

"Perhaps there is a witch somewhere," he said, "who is hurting your judgement."

"It is understandable," said Erik, kindly, "that you believe the world is full of witches. But it is not."

Erik was realizing, perhaps for the first time, that there were people in the world that he loved. He loved his children—these seven sons and daughters—despite such childish ways as their belief in witches. You probably did not even know that he had children, since I never mentioned them before. But he never mentioned them either. They were not an essential part of his life. And there's nothing I can do about that.

But now here he was suddenly feeling all this love for them. What makes a father who didn't seem to love his children before suddenly love them now?

The old king was sad to feel such love and yet have to leave. But what else was there to do? Love meant weakness, and weakness meant retirement, across the sea. Still, he wanted to leave some words to heed. He believed there might be some, and so he waited, and finally spoke.

"I'll say only this. Don't ever be cruel to the old or to the infirm—be he a man or a beast. Or a bird. Those who have seen so much do not deserve your cruelty. And if they could fight back, they would have every right to defeat you. And perhaps they would defeat you.

For that is what happened to me."

And so, just after midnight, the former tyrant took his leave of these sons and daughters he loved. The seven Haralds waded down into the icy surf and pushed off their father's boats and then they walked back up the hill and into the country of Norway, ready to prove with power of arms that it could be Viking again, not Christian. Ruled by Viking gods.

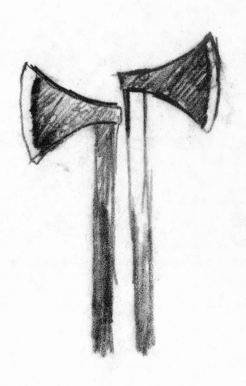

3

The Story

ROLF AND RAT-A-TASK had been walking for awhile—or rather, Rolf did the walking, though the squirrel on his shoulder led the way—through trees that rose up into the darkness like sentinels, sometimes even like silent kings. The boy realized that they were following the sound of a river, coming nearer and nearer to its bank. Rat-A-Task had promised to tell him more about where they were going. It took the squirrel awhile to get around to it, since he was mostly interested in telling the whole story of his life, pretending there was more to it than a few weeks of nesting in the rafters of a house. But, then again, there *was* more to it, since the squirrel could barely distinguish between the story of his own life and the stories he'd been told *in* his life. So Rolf tried to be patient and eventually the squirrel began.

"There is a rumour," said Rat-A-Task, "or a story rather, since a story is larger and older than a rumour, and this was an old rumour. A story then, whispered for generations among the squirrel population, about how there was once a place called the Tree of the World, that was bigger than everything we have ever seen. It was so big, it actually connected the world we know with the world of the gods. Like a bridge, really, except a bridge that grew up and down, and had branches, rather than a fallen tree that served as a more conventional bridge across a river."

Rolf's head was swirling, already full of questions about giant trees and bridges and the world of the gods. But he could not make any of his questions into a single word sentence and anyway, the squirrel was going on with his tale.

"Something happened," said the squirrel. "A long time ago. So my mother told me, if you must know, and her mother told her and her mother told her, etcetera. As I told you, squirrels are very scholarly creatures."

"What?" asked Rolf. Meaning: What happened?

"The Tree of the World fell to the ground and severed the bridge between earth and heaven. Some say it was felled with an axe. Some say the gods pushed it over because they didn't like the idea of people being able to come up and knock on the door of their great feasting hall. But others say that the Tree of the World wasn't so much a bridge to the world of the gods as a foundation for it. They say that the world of the gods rested in the tree's upper branches. And one day the tree got knocked over somehow. And after that the gods were never seen or heard from, ever again."

"Wow," said Rolf, who hadn't even known he knew that word.

"But there's a rumour," said the squirrel. "A rumour being whispered in all the rafters of the land. It says that the tree that once fell is growing again. That it has been growing for some years now. That it has been growing from a single seed buried far beneath the earth by a squirrel. And if the Tree of the World is re-growing, then so too must be the pantheon of the gods.

"But the important thing," continued Rat-A-Task to Rolf, "is the fact that, aside from the unknown little hero who planted that seed, there is *another* important squirrel, a very important squirrel, a little squirrel that runs up and down the Tree of the World, delivering messages from top to bottom and bottom to top."

"Messages?" asked Rolf, still full of awe.

"What messages, you ask?" replied the squirrel. "What does it even matter what messages? It is an honourable position, depicted in the pantheon, depicted in the lore! I'll tell you what I think, though." Here he became very conspiratorial, on Rolf's shoulder, looking around for prying ears and leaning in, clinging to the edge of the boy's giant ear. "I have a hunch. I can only imagine the messages had to do with the care and maintenance of the tree. And that the squirrel who once bore this responsibility did his job very poorly, because he failed to stop that first falling tree! And so!" And here he stretched up to his full tiny height, like a tiny commander, and waved his paw defiantly as if it were a single finger. "I can tell you who has the smarts and the stamina to do this job now!"

"You!" said Rolf.

"Precisely," answered Rat-A-Task. "And I can't imagine what a squirrel of a Tree of the World needs more than a powerful giant by his side, to help him make his case!"

"Yes," said Rolf. He was feeling something growing in his chest. He had been promised an adventure, and oh yes, this was going to be an adventure. He felt such excitement that he was about to let out a whoop. A big whoop. A whoop that would probably have frightened the little red squirrel perched on his shoulder.

But something stopped him. He had been striding through the dark woods, barely paying attention to his surroundings, hardly hearing the gurgling of the hidden river somewhere off to their right, in thrall to Rat-A-Task's words. But then a living thing came into his field of vision, not far ahead of him in the gloom.

4

A Man in the Woods

THERE WAS A HORSE standing there in the woods, some distance away, nickering and blowing among the trees. Rolf saw it and stopped and drew in his breath, and the sound of the breath cut short the chattering of the squirrel. Suddenly the two of them, giant and furry red rodent, were just as still and silent as the trees around them.

Near the nickering horse, a man was down on one knee, facing away from them, carving something into the face of a trunk. Rolf wondered whether such carving could hurt the tree. He remembered how he had uprooted a tree not long ago and used it in battle. He resolved never to do such a thing again.

The man was thickset and ugly. For a moment—just a moment—Rolf thought it was The Beaky kneeling

33

there, even though The Beaky was not thickset and ugly but rather thin and—well, you know what I'm getting at. I don't want to say The Beaky was handsome, because that might be taking it a little too far. But the reason Rolf thought it might have been The Beaky was because this man appeared to have found himself a beak. In the shadows, Rolf could see there was something protruding from the middle of his head.

But then Rolf saw that it wasn't a beak at all, but rather a horn, coming out of the centre of his helmet in the front. Why would someone—presumably a Viking—wear a single horn in the centre of his helmet? It seemed dangerous, like it could poke a person's eye out. Like it could be really funny until someone loses an eye.

The man completed his carving. He rose and turned. Rat-A-Task tucked himself into Rolf's sweater and the boy, though he was quite a distance away from the stranger, stood straight as he could and tried to pretend he was just another tree in the darkness.

It seemed to work. The man stood for a long moment, gazing straight at him. But there was a faraway look in his eyes and, after another moment, Rolf could see the unmistakable gleam of tears.

Then the man plodded wearily over to his horse, mounted it, and rode away to the south.

When he was gone, Rat-A-Task crawled back out onto Rolf's shoulder. "I want to know what that man carved on the tree. Do you?"

Rolf was so puffed up with curiosity, he thought his feet might come off the ground. He nodded, waded through the snow over to the tree, and crouched low to peer at the markings that had split their way through the bark to the lighter wood beneath.

Egil am I,
Lost to the fire
That burbled over
Iceland's earth.
Driven from Norway,
Now I return
To this land
Of my versing's birth

Though Erik Blood-Axe
Has banished me,
Only here can my heart
Speak its poetry,
Only here can I finally
Know my worth.

"Egil," said Rolf, full of wonder. "Egil . . ."

"I've never heard of him," said Rat-A-Task. "Banished by Erik Blood-Axe, was he?"

"Banished," repeated Rolf. He felt that one word, "banished," was full of drama and the mystery of a far-away world full of adventures that make up the stuff of great stories. Banished.

He was confused about one thing though. "Lost?" he asked.

"Lost to the fire that burbled over Iceland," said the squirrel. And then continued like the scholarly squirrel he was. "Iceland. An island to the west, in the middle of the Atlantic Ocean. Not icy at all. In fact it's green. If fire burbled there, though, it sounds to me like he was lost to a volcanic eruption."

"How?" asked Rolf.

"How what?" replied the squirrel. And then he understood. "How could one man be both lost to a far-away eruption and also here in Norway? It is indeed a paradox." He wrinkled up his nose. "Though I suspect a scholarly squirrel might unravel it."

"Yes," said Rolf.

Rat-A-Task scrunched up his face and thought a little more. Then suddenly his paw went up like a single finger making a point. "I have it," he said. "I suspect he lost something there that makes him feel as if he himself were dead."

"Who?" asked Rolf.

"How can you assume it's a who?" replied the squirrel. "If I had lost something that made me feel I was dead, I would have to say it was 'the plan!' or 'my ambition!' or, I suppose, 'my superior intellect!' Though how my superior intellect could ever be lost, I cannot say. But I cannot think what else it could be, and I certainly cannot imagine a *who*."

Rolf shook his giant head, startling the squirrel,

who thought for a moment he was going to get shaken off his perch. Rolf did not notice, though; he was too busy thinking. There was something about the sadness of this man in the woods, even at a distance, that reminded him of his own father.

And then, for a brief moment, he thought of his mother.

"Family," he said, finally.

"Uh-huh," said the squirrel, pretending to consider what he clearly thought was a ridiculous idea. "It is an interesting theory. But you might note how I just lost my whole family and you don't see me shedding any tears. Then again, I suppose we all just left the nest, which is what we were meant to do. Nobody died."

"No," said Rolf.

"You think this man had a family and they died. Yes," the squirrel sighed. "Humans are so emotional. And so are giants too, I see. As explanations go, it's not as exciting as I'd hoped, but that's probably it."

Rolf was a little surprised by the coldness of his friend, but he was too polite to make any protest as Rat-A-Task went on. "There's some good news, though. Surely this man will be happy to hear how Erik Blood-Axe has been defeated in battle and he's probably well on his way to . . ."

"Scotland," said Rolf, remembering what the old king had said on the Field of Snorre.

"Scotland," repeated the squirrel. "Indeed."

As they strode on, Rolf spoke the words again and

again inside his head, trying to commit them to memory. For it has to be said that, though Rolf spoke in single words, the thoughts in his head made markedly more. He wondered too, as he walked, whether he would ever meet this man again.

But as the small hours of the night gave way to the darkest darkness before the dawn, Rolf forgot all about Egil the Poet, at least for the moment, as he began to suspect they were getting closer to their destination.

5

The Tree

"IT'S JUST BEYOND that high plateau," said Rat-A-Task. "Do you see the plateau? Way up there?"

It was morning. Though the sky was overcast, still the light from the waterfall made Rolf blink and shield his eyes. He was standing about a hundred feet away from a sheer rock face that came up out of the ground as if someone had once tried to push the earth apart in this very spot. The cliff stretched as far as the eye could see on either side of him. There was no way around it. And it rose so high as to disappear into the cloud bank that covered the world. Almost directly in front of him, a thin groove ran down the face, carved there over centuries by the single pearl-coloured ribbon of water that poured from a place above the clouds and burbled and sang as it kissed the

39

river below. The waterfall was an enormous, powerful thing, but the hugeness of the cliff made it seem as delicate as string spun from spider thread. Rolf did not think the natural formations of the earth could be so big. Already he was feeling not so much like a giant anymore.

"Don't you see the plateau?" asked the squirrel.

"Where?" Rolf asked.

"Look between the falling water."

Rolf was wondering how he was supposed to look between water.

"Up there!" said the squirrel. "You'll see. Behind the face of the rock behind the waterfall. My mother told me. Way up there, the falling water peeled away a part of the rock, creating a crevice, big enough for even you to fit through."

Rolf was still doubtful. What if all these things that Rat-A-Task had been told by his mother were not true? After all, she was just a mother squirrel in a nest, doing the best she could, telling stories to her children so they might fall asleep and give her a bit of peace. What if Rolf were to climb all that way up to where the squirrel was pointing, only to find more rock behind all that rock? And then, once he was up there and had to come back down, what if he learned he was afraid of heights?

That would be very, very bad.

But Rat-A-Task was sure of himself. "Just climb," he said. "And then you'll see."

Rolf took a deep breath. "Now?" he asked.

"Yes! Now! So what are you waiting for? Climb!"

Rolf started to walk toward the waterfall. He looked up—way, way up—and didn't want to be afraid. So he shut down his thoughts and broke into a run.

"What are you doing?" asked the startled squirrel as he bounced up and down on Rolf's shoulder.

"Running," said Rolf and closed his eyes.

"I can see that you're running! Why are you running?"

And then Rat-A-Task saw that Rolf's eyes were closed. "Now what are you doing?" he chittered. "Are you insane?"

And then the squirrel could chitter no longer, his teeth were chattering so much. Rolf covered the last hundred yards with speed that might after all be expected from a giant, opened his eyes at the last moment, leapt up onto the rock face, and held.

"That was simply not logical or necessary!" cried Rat-A-Task, finally. "We're not in that much of a hurry! We've got plenty of time! I'll thank you to be more careful the rest of the way!"

Rolf ignored his little friend. He climbed as if his life depended on it. He climbed as if he'd been doing it all his life. He climbed through the morning as fast as he'd walked through the night.

As he climbed, Rolf realized it wasn't, after all, the first time. Once, when he was small, he had climbed up onto the roof of the little house with the red-painted door and then was afraid to climb back down. His father had to come up and get him. Rolf clasped his hands around his father's neck and held on for dear life as they descended. He wondered now, as he climbed, whether he had weighed as little as this squirrel did, to his father. Probably not. Probably it was difficult for his father to carry him down.

He was a good father.

Wasn't he?

And Rolf was still small. He was a small boy in a giant's body. And he knew how to climb up but maybe not down again. He had a feeling this would not be the first time he'd know how to do the first half of something but not the second.

Still, he climbed like he was born to it, like it was written in the giant's genetic code (to use a bit of learning from your latter day). And maybe it was. I know for a fact that I would not be able to climb like that. Why do readers of stories always think they'll be just like the brave one? Maybe they don't, maybe not always. I know that I'd run in the opposite direction from that cliff. Or else I'd sit at the bottom and wait for whoever goes up to come back down, staring at the crows in the trees on the opposite bank. That's what I'd do.

On the way up, alongside the waterfall, Rolf felt the spray against his face. He climbed for a long time, trying not to think of the ache he felt in his shoulders and his legs. He knew he was strong and would not slip. Unless, of course . . .

Rolf's right hand closed over a rock that came away from the cliff and so he lost his balance, just like that. His left hand could not hold him and he leaned right back into the sky. And fell. The river was far below him. He clutched, desperately, grasping for anything. His hat flew off his head and was gone. His fingers closed over a sapling, hanging onto the cliff by its roots. It was very thin, with leaves as tiny and delicate as baby's breath. There was no soil to hold it to the water-smooth face—absolutely no way it was going to bear the giant boy's weight. Rolf should have been falling backwards toward the earth with a squirrel screaming in his ear.

But the sapling held him. And it had all happened so fast, Rat-A-Task was unaware anything had gone awry. Rolf hung there, clinging to a tiny branch, swinging sky high, defying all logic, while a wind swept down from above and whistled in his ears.

He realized he was not afraid.

Because then he saw. This wasn't a tiny dry sapling growing hopelessly against the smooth cliff wall, but rather the last, thinnest tip of a branch that had made its way along the rock face in search of more sunlight. It was tougher than it looked. As Rolf gripped and held, he saw that this green sinew grew out of another sinew, a thicker sinew, which itself grew out of a bark-coated branch, and that branch snaked through a tiny crevice in the wall and disappeared into the darkness behind it.

There was something behind the cliff. And Rolf was swinging lightly back and forth, surprised by what he had just discovered.

"Are you falling?" asked the squirrel, suddenly aware that something was amiss. "Are you falling? What's happening?"

"No," said Rolf.

"Then why are you stopping?" shouted the squirrel. "Don't give up now! We're almost there!"

And Rolf didn't say anything because he knew it was true.

And then, as he continued to climb, Rolf realized that the falling water was no longer on either side of him, but rather behind him, tickling his neck and his back with its spray. When he looked straight up, he could just see the top of the cliff, from where it poured over. As he climbed closer to it, he sensed that it would fall closer and closer to him, until he was right inside the rush. He could feel it happening already.

Finally, Rolf grasped a rock that held tight to the edge of a plateau, and he pulled himself up and onto a surface that was finally, thankfully, level with the sky. Though the plateau was so slippery from constant contact with water, he nearly slid off. Still, he held, and lay there panting, feet sticking out over the void, and listened for the first time to the roar of the falling water hitting the river far below.

Rat-A-Task, for his part, was dancing a sophisticated

squirrel dance on Rolf's back. Three steps to the left, three to the right, swish swish goes the tail, nod the head twice, and then start the whole thing all over again. He was pointing to a wide crevice behind Rolf's head, opening into the darkness, crammed with branches creeping their way toward the light. Still big enough for a small giant to fit through.

"It's there!" the squirrel shouted, triumphantly. "It's really there!" And then he looked impatiently down at Rolf, who was too exhausted to feel excitement. Though he did feel relief.

"You can rest in a minute," said Rat-A-Task. "Let's go in."

A few minutes later, Rolf understood why Rat-A-Task knew he would love it here.

Because you could never be lonely here.

The tree. When they climbed through the crevice, they found themselves in the middle of its immensity. Below them, it stretched much farther than the distance they'd climbed up the cliff; above them, it stretched high through a break in the clouds. Before them, it stretched out as if the whole world hung like a hammock from a limb, or as if the world sat on top of it like a bird's nest on a branch. Or as if the world grew out of it like a mushroom from the bark. All these things were possible, but the tree was so large it was

45

impossible to say which was the correct way of seeing it.

Rat-A-Task said, "See how the world is bigger than you ever thought?"

"Yes," said Rolf, who truly did.

A lonely young giant boy could never be lonely here. Even the leaves spoke to him. Or so it seemed. They whispered as he climbed by, up, down, sideways, he could go in any direction, it was so big. They swished past his ears. Green leaves of enormous size, flat and round, coming to a delicate point—not at all like the needles that covered the trees of Norway. Not like the bare trees too that reached for the sky with naked twigs like Morton's broken wings. Rolf wondered whether all those bare trees were supposed to look like this.

And the trunk felt warm as he held it. Warmth that came from within. And he felt an even stronger heat touching the top of his head. So he looked up and saw the sun. Or thought he saw until he realized it was just bright reflecting light from the sun, bouncing off a million leaves to glimmer and blaze in his eyes. The sun itself was not there, directly overhead, but rather somewhere to the east, behind the clouds. It was morning and the sun had just risen and had some way to come before it would emerge from among the snarling branches overhead. The sky was blue up there though, and so the leaves saw the sun, no question about that. It was as if the clouds had parted to let the tree grow through. And the tree had obliged.

It was clear that this tree was not finished with its

growing. Rolf could feel the bark expand, little by little, beneath his hands. A tree that grew so fast you could almost see it.

The main simple thing Rolf loved about this tree though was just the way it made him feel small. Its limbs and branches held him in their embrace and he felt like he could hang from them forever and they would never grow tired. In the hours he spent lost in the fun of that tree, climbing, with the squirrel silent and awed by his ear, Rolf felt the memories of younger days return and expand within him until they too were giant. Sweet and bitter reminders of the days he had shared sitting under bushes with his sister.

Freya . . .

"Wait here," the squirrel said suddenly, unexpectedly. "I'll be back."

And then he skittered off Rolf's shoulder and onto the trunk.

"Wait!" called Rolf.

"What?" asked the squirrel, suddenly impatient.

Rolf had a thousand questions. He had his arm draped over a branch and was hanging there, like a gorilla, dazed and gazing down at Rat, who had skittered several yards down the trunk and had turned halfway back toward him, tail twitching.

Rolf could not think of anything to ask.

"See?" said the squirrel. "You thought *that* was the world: That puny little village of Trondheim in the narrow strip of land called Norway with its silly little battles between brothers over quaint little matters such as kingship. But *this*, my friend," and here he swooped his tail in a large and generous circle, nearly tripping himself in the process (which, since he was already clinging sideways to the trunk would have sent him hurtling down into the millions of leaves below), "*this* is the world. This tree holds up your world and more besides. Down below, in the depths, it holds the world below the world, where the dwarves once kept their forges but have long stayed silent. Above our heads, cradled in the highest branches, you might one day—who knows?—find the empty chambers of the gods. Everything is being prepared, my friend. Everything is being prepared."

Prepared for what? Rolf wanted to ask, but Rat was in a hurry. "Can I go now?" he asked sarcastically. Rolf nodded his head and the squirrel turned and went. He ran down the tree as if it were flat as the land and disappeared.

Rolf swung himself up onto a limb and sat in the corner where it joined the trunk. He was alone, but he did not feel alone. Bliss. Just in front of him, a small branch was growing from the limb with a tiny leaf, smaller even than Rat-A-Task. Like all the rest, this leaf seemed to be whispering. Rolf leaned in close with his ear to listen.

"My name is Idun," it whispered distinctly. "I'm a leaf. Be careful. I am young and delicate. I've got my whole life ahead of me."

"I will," whispered Rolf, who was barely even aware that he spoke, much less spoke two words. "I will be careful."

It is difficult to say how long the squirrel was gone. For Rolf, time passed in shimmers of leafy beauty, basking in the protection of his new friend. He watched and listened. A lizard crawled up the vast trunk, ignoring him. Idun whispered. A bird landed on a nearby limb—speckled with a plume that shot from the top of its head like fireworks. It ignored him too, groomed its plume, and then flew off, zigzagging down into the depths beyond his sight, where he saw other climbing creatures, silent, content, busy, foraging.

Here was a home like he had never seen.

He wanted to stay.

He wanted to stay forever.

A night went by, and morning came. Sap oozed from the trunk. Idun encouraged Rolf to take some and eat it. She was speaking with his best interest in mind. The sap was like sweet and salt together. He liked it and ate some more. The tree didn't seem to mind.

Finally Rat-A-Task returned, looking dejected.

"Me," said the squirrel. "Such feelings I have. I can't even put a name to them."

"What?" asked Rolf. He was worried for his friend, not accustomed to Rat being anything other than bursting with confidence.

"I met him," said the squirrel. "He exists, just like

my mother told me. Down there, curled around the roots of the tree."

"Who?" asked Rolf.

"But he rejected me," said Rat, ignoring the question. "I offered my services. The position is *clearly* unfilled. I haven't seen any other squirrel go running up and down the tree. Have you?"

"No," said Rolf, who had not seen any other squirrel at all.

"But still, he laughed at me," said the squirrel. "He rejected my case."

"Who?" Rolf tried again.

"The Dreki," said Rat. "Who else?"

"Dreki?" Rolf gasped. Rat had never mentioned this before, so it certainly wasn't fair for him to speak as if it was obvious. Rolf had heard of creatures with such a name, in fireside tales told by his father on spooky nights, but his father had also assured him that nobody had seen such creatures for hundreds of years. Only their bones, buried in the ground and scattered about.

But I have to stop here and explain what a Dreki is. Rolf was familiar with the term, but if he was going to be honest he would have had to admit he wasn't exactly sure what it was, in spite of the tales told by his father. It's hard to hold a picture of the Dreki in your mind. There are those who have even written big books about it who were never sure what a Dreki actually was.

The fact is—at least maybe—that a Dreki is very

large, or, if it's not large we can at least agree that it takes up a lot of space and leave it at that. And it is also very smart and very, very ugly. That much is certain. That much we can agree on. It also reportedly has teeth and scales and a tail, and you could never see the whole of it even if it presented itself to you entirely. Not because it's large, necessarily, but rather because it is well versed in the art of concealment. Also, the Dreki is born from the fire that comes out of a crack in the earth, and it has the ability to generate this same volcanic fire within its lungs. In other words, it breathes fire. In short, it is like a dragon. But apparently not *exactly* like a dragon, which is why we will agree to call it a Dreki. For one thing, it is apparently very fat . . . or else it is very thin. And I've heard that it is very small and only makes itself *seem* like it's very big. Unless it's the other way around. But that sounds impossible to me. And most rumours you hear saying the Dreki doesn't really exist were likely started by the Dreki.

And, like a dragon, it is always difficult to tell whether its intentions are good or bad. Wisdom always comes at a price because a Dreki also knows everything. If you think a squirrel is a know-it-all, you should try talking to a Dreki.

In short, the more you try and describe a Dreki, the more uncertain you become, which puts you at a distinct disadvantage when you're up against the Dreki. And of course the Dreki would not have it any other way. It likes to have the upper hand in an argument.

I, for one, am afraid of the Dreki (even now) and the chaos it can inspire. Gives me the shivers just to write about it, gives me the heebie-jeebies, especially considering how late it is. It *is* getting rather late. I thought last time that I had stayed up late, but this time I've replaced the candle with an oil lamp, and such things can burn for hours without having to be replaced. A marvellous technological leap, the oil lamp.

Rat-A-Task was continuing to speak about his meeting with the Dreki, which, Rolf had the impression, was wrapped around the roots at the bottom of the Tree of the World. He listened, more than a little unnerved.

"I even told the Dreki I had brought you! *You!* But he laughed at me. 'What do you know of the destiny of the Tree of the World,' he asked me, 'little newborn mammal creature?' No, he thinks you won't do, that you can't do it. He said you were just a little boy!"

"What?" asked Rolf, meaning to ask what the squirrel had in mind for Rolf to do that the Dreki didn't think he could do.

But, as usual, Rat ignored him and went on. "And he said that I was just a boy too! But we'll show him. Come on."

And the squirrel scurried back up onto Rolf's shoulder.

6

The Task

ROLF WAS HAPPY to have inspired such confidence in the little squirrel, who was even now pointing up and out, toward the crevice and the plateau and the world outside. But he also felt worried about the tree, and the authority of the Dreki. He felt suddenly scared that he might not be allowed to stay in this place that was more beautiful even than Freya's wings. There were many mixed emotions inside him, not least a touch of indignation at being found unworthy by a creature who had never even met him.

"Where?" he asked. Meaning: Where are we going?

"We must find more!" said Rat-A-Task. "More like you! That's what he says you can't do! He says you can't be a leader of giants. But I say you can! I say you can lead! I don't have any choice, really, in thinking that, since you're the only giant I know. But with me at your ear, I'm confident you can do anything! I've got the brains and you've got the brawn. The brains!" He pointed with his paw at his own little head. "And the brawn!" He grasped a lock of hair that fell by Rolf's ear and gave it a playful tug. And then he conducted another jaunty little squirrel dance on the giant boy's shoulder.

Rolf wanted to ask why he was suddenly being asked to lead a group of giants. The squirrel had spoken before about *finding* giants, but even that had been mysterious. Rolf didn't even think there were any giants in the world, other than himself. His big, oafish, clumsy self. But the squirrel was still chittering.

"They must be out there, in the landscape. Do you know any? From that village where you come from? No, of course you don't. I can tell by that permanent lonesome expression you've got. I thought I would have wiped that clean by now. Well, one thing is certain. We must find more."

"Why?" asked Rolf.

"Isn't it obvious?" asked the squirrel. "We need an army!"

"Army," repeated Rolf, puzzled.

"A giant army! There aren't any creatures who appreciate beauty more than the giants. I don't know why. Perhaps it's because you're all so very ugly. Is that why?"

Rolf shrugged. No one had ever called him ugly

before. Clumsy, yes. Oafish. But ugly? Was this how friends described friends?

Rat continued, abruptly changing the subject. "Or would you rather let the enemies of this tree come and chop it down?"

Rolf gasped.

"Because that is what they will do," said the squirrel, "if we do not stop them."

"Them?" asked Rolf. "Who?"

"Think about it," said the squirrel. "If the tree is growing again, and the protectors of the tree—I mean the giants—are growing again, then it's likely the enemies of this tree are growing again too. And we have to guard against them even if we don't know who they are!"

"Right!" said Rolf with conviction. Although it also occurred to him that there was nothing scarier than wanting to guard against an enemy without even knowing who that enemy was.

"A place like this," explained the squirrel, "is like a bridge between several worlds. Really, it's more like a ladder, but it's better for now to think of it as a bridge. You might think that's a good thing. But imagine you're standing on a beautiful stone bridge, hundreds of years old. On either side, there are two armies gathering. The only thing they hate more than one another is the bridge that links them."

"But—" said Rolf. He didn't quite understand. Rat had already said the tree held up the worlds. If that were true, then it wasn't really accurate to say the tribes were on either side of the bridge. If that were true, then the tribes were perched right there on the bridge itself. And if someone destroyed a bridge like that, wouldn't they also destroy the tribes too, both together?

It was all too confusing. Rolf decided that he probably just didn't understand. He was, after all, only nine years old, and this little squirrel knew so much more about the world than he did.

They climbed over the last branches, through the crevice, and out onto the plateau. And then they looked through the stream of water out over the cloud-shadowed snow-covered land.

Rolf was ready to go whichever direction this squirrel pointed, if it meant hope for the tree. From the source of the wind to the path of the sun, and the glow of the moon on the face of a wall, everything in nature has a guide. On this morning, Rolf decided that he had a guide too, small enough to curl around his ear. A guide and an ally, in search of an army of giants. He would overcome his shyness and address himself to these fellow giants, if they allowed themselves to be found, even if the idea seemed unpleasant to him, which it did.

He looked out through the spray. Once his eyes adjusted, it was as if the water wasn't there. He looked as far as he could see and still he could not see his little house out there, or even the village of Trondheim.

All there was to see was a forest, shrouded in cloud, that roamed far to the north and the south and the east. Had he really travelled so far already? Would he ever be able to find his way home?

He tried to tell himself that he didn't want to go home. Perhaps it was true what Rat had said about Freya coldly leaving him. But the squirrel had not been completely friend-like already. Was it possible he'd told Rolf some things that weren't necessarily true? Was it possible that Freya was alone somewhere, feeling bereft and full of grief?

Then again, had Freya not gotten herself into that whole situation because she was also ambitious? Was she not like this squirrel then? Tough and ambitious and not at all like the *new* friend Rolf had made?

Idun, a delicate little leaf. He'd only just met her, but he already knew. Idun kept his best interests in mind. Idun would never say Rolf was ugly. Idun would never say he was clumsy. Idun would never call him an oaf. All Idun wanted was his friendship and his company. Well, he would give her his friendship. And he would give her his company. He would do what Rat asked him to do, not for Rat, but for the little leaf who was his new friend.

They were about to begin their descent down the cliff. In fact, Rolf had pulled himself over the edge and was holding with one hand on the jagged outcrop while his feet tried to find some purchase below, when something caught his eye down there, behind him and below him, through the water and the spray.

He turned his head around, as far as he could, to look, slipping a bit as he did. Far below him he saw a scrum of men—warriors it seemed, even from this height—standing in a tight circle, looking inward, with their hands pointing to the centre, touching some gleaming thing. A sword perhaps. Seven warriors and a single sword. Were they fighting over it? No. Perhaps they were making some kind of pact.

Rolf turned again to look, craning his neck. His hand slipped, just like before, only this time there was no sapling to grasp and hold. And so he fell. For real this time. He fell straight back into space. Instinct told him, once he began to fall, that he should push himself with his feet as far away from the face of the cliff as he could get. So he arced backwards through the spray of the water to the other side, soaked and hurtling straight down, as little stones fell around him, scuffed away from the wall.

But Rolf was not afraid.

Though Rat-A-Task screamed and cursed and skittered into his sweater, Rolf did not even think he made a sound. He was too busy imagining instead about how this was what it felt like for his sister to fly. This hurtling. For the moment, Rolf forgot all about the anger and resentment he felt and wondered if this was really what it was like. No doubt there was a difference between going straight up and going straight down. But he felt, for his purposes anyway, it did not matter. It helped him to understand his sister at least a little bit. What fun it must have been.

Rolf thought maybe one day he could tell Freya that he had once flown like her. And since he also thought this was his last ever thought, he held onto it like a cherished thing as he fell, knowing he would die with his sister's memory curled inside his thoughts.

Like the squirrel now screaming and holding on for dear life within his shirt.

7

Captured

ROLF AWOKE to the flicker of light touching his sore eye. His back hurt. He was, in fact, stiff and sore all over. He was cold and his clothes were wet. There was a fire there, built near him, but when he tried to move closer to the heat of the flames, he found he could not budge. Something was preventing him. Nearby, icicles hung from the bank of the river and dripped toward the rushing surface, as if longing to join the river in its whirling.

"Don't move," Rolf heard a voice say. Quiet, and very close. "And listen carefully."

The voice was familiar, but he could not place it. It was very close. Freya? Father? No, neither of them spoke like that. The voice was small. Like the rustling of dry leaves in his ear.

His head was throbbing and his right ear was bothering him, as if something was stuck to it, clutching it. He tried to lift his hand to scratch it, but he found he could not do that either.

"Don't move!" the voice said again. "I want a chance to talk to you before they realize you're awake. It's no use anyway. They've got you tied up."

So that was it. He was tied up. It made him want to struggle but the voice said again, "Don't." And then went on. "You think you're in a bind, but this will come around to our advantage. You'll see."

Rolf was trying to think. The sky above his face was growing dark and his head would not cease its throbbing. His memory was hazy. Was this the Field of Snorre? Had they been defeated and captured by the tyrant King Erik Blood-Axe? Was Freya in trouble? Was she nearby? Also captured? He felt instinctively that she was in trouble. But who was talking to him? Where was the voice coming from? Was it hidden? Did it belong to a rescuer?

He struggled again for a moment and then remembered. No. Freya was safe. Rolf had given Morton's wings to her and she had gotten away. And then come back. He remembered a flash of wings. A hole in the sky where the sun came through. A hole in the sky where Freya came through.

A hole in the sky that the tree grew through.

The tree.

The Tree. Of the World.

Rolf remembered. He had fallen from the flat face of the cliff, way up high. He'd believed it was the end of his life. He'd pretended he was going to fly, to give himself something to do while he was dying. He'd been reminded of Freya as he fell, and that had made him happy, though he'd missed her as he fell, he'd missed her *so much*. When he hit the water, he'd had just enough time to wonder whether he could swim before the big rock loomed and ended his speculation.

Now he became aware of figures beyond the flicker of fire. His captors. He overheard them. They were having an argument. The argument seemed to be about him.

"This giant," someone was saying. "He is the sign. Just like what father said he saw on the Field of Snorre. If the giants have returned, then so have the gods."

"But the giants are the *enemies* of the gods," said someone else, who sounded like he wasn't accustomed to anyone questioning his authority.

"So?" said the other, more tremulous but filled with certainty. "They're still proof of one another."

It sounded like a girl's voice, though Rolf was not sure, because she seemed to be lowering her tone, trying to sound like a boy.

The girl/boy went on. "Bees have terrible stingers, but they're still the best sign of flowers. If you see a bee, you know there must be a flower out there somewhere."

"What do flowers have to do with anything?"

"Nothing! I'm just saying!"

"I still don't believe a giant is a good sign of anything."

"Well, you're just a terrible pessimist."

"You're just a terrible optimist."

"But this giant looks like he's just a little boy."

"He's still a giant."

"But he's a boy giant. If the giants are children, then maybe the gods that are out there are children too."

"That's just ridiculous. That's a ridiculous theory. Giants are stupid and gods can't be children because—because they're gods! And anyway, giants are the enemies of the gods."

"You said that already."

I have to leave the voices for the moment and explain a part of this story that I have not yet spoken of, in part because I don't like it, but also because, so far, Rolf and Freya have remained blissfully ignorant of certain cold, hard facts concerning their separate natures. According to Viking lore (and please forgive me for a moment while I roll my eyes far up into my head, entertaining the thought that "lore" has engendered more "war" than your average rhyming couplet), according to Viking lore (from which Freya and Rolf had been shielded by a—really—wise and judicious father), gods and giants are irreconcilable enemies who generally live in different worlds. This was always the case. The giants are strong and have long memories, but the gods traditionally consider them to be inferior beings. The gods, in fact, have been reported many times to have tricked the giants into performing difficult tasks for them—like designing and building walls and castles—

and then slipping out of whatever deal they made for payment. "That's not fair," you might say. And you'd be right. Mind you, it's also true that giants are traditionally known to ask for impossible fees in exchange for their work, like somebody's daughter in marriage or a piece of the sun or something. The giants tend to be naive that way—they speak directly of their heart's desire and expect to be told, as they were by their parents, whether or not they can have it. But instead of negotiating, instead of being straight up and telling this or that giant that he can't have this daughter or that immense store of riches, instead of saying, "Look here, be reasonable, Orf. You can't have the goddess Freyja; anyway she's already betrothed; how about instead I give you 217 pieces of gold?" Instead of doing any of that, the wily gods (according to legend, according to "lore") just say, "Sure thing." And so this or that giant builds the wall or the castle, the feasting table of Valhalla, or even the great hall itself. And when he's done and comes to collect his fee, the gods send out one of their own to trick him. Usually to kill him. They tell themselves he deserves to be punished for expecting a large payment for such a minor and insignificant task as—for example—building a bridge over the ocean. It makes me quiver with rage to think about it. And since quivering is yet another sign of weakness, it makes me embarrassed as well. But what can I do? It's appalling. It's unjust! And for any of you who think myths and legends are all about how gallant this or that god has been, you should look again at the behaviour of the gods toward the giants. Because traditionally, at least according to *lore*, they have not been very nice. To put it mildly . . .

The giants haven't been very nice either, but generally only after they've been betrayed, hard done by, screwed over, if I may use an expression from your day.

Rolf didn't know any of this. Neither did Freya. Their father never told them. And even if Freya had been bad-tempered from time to time about Rolf's clumsiness, she would never have betrayed him or tried to get something from him for nothing. Not in any way. I can tell you that for a fact. Even if she herself is not present in this story in which Rolf has been tied up and held captive, you can be sure that if she knew about it, she would be here in a flash.

Still, imagine what it must have been like for Rolf in that situation: There he was, all tied up, not knowing where he was, not knowing who had captured him, listening to unfamiliar voices argue about whether he was stupid or dangerous or a sign of something, or a child or a giant or a bee in a flower. It was all very confusing. Rolf as a sign of the return of the gods. As a citizen of Norway in 934, Rolf wasn't even sure he believed in the gods anymore. And he didn't know anyone who did. These voices though, they sure sounded like they believed in something.

You may have gleaned by now that Rolf's captors were the sons and daughters of Erik Blood-Axe. And since these sons and daughters were steeped in this same "lore" that I have just related, they were biased in favour of the gods. And so they were concerned about the presence of a giant in their midst. But also excited, since a giant would seem to confirm the possibility of gods. The eldest Harald was playing devil's advocate, arguing against anyone else who spoke up—especially the second eldest, who was in fact a daughter and not a son—but really he was just as excited by this possibility as the rest.

The Haralds went on, still very much overheard by Rolf.

"Is it not said," asked the second eldest, "by those who look at the stars and think about the future, that the gods would be slowly reborn, right here, in our towns and villages, and they would grow among us? Has it not been said that we would nurture them and one day they would rebuild their upper realm and reclaim their rightful place above the clouds?"

"Of course," said the eldest. "Of course all these things are told. At least for those who listen."

"Is it not then a matter of some urgency?" asked the second eldest. "Do not such stories make the gods sound childlike and vulnerable, at least in the beginning? And what's more, with a Christian king of Norway and crosses popping up all over the land, could the gods not just whither away, like flowers without water?"

"There you go again," said the eldest. "Comparing gods and flowers. You can't just go and compare gods and flowers all the time! It's embarrassing! What kind of Viking do you think you are?"

"I'm just trying to convey the urgency of the situation!" protested the second eldest.

"Talking about pretty flowers," said the eldest, "hardly conveys the urgency of any situation, especially to Vikings. I'm willing to bet you've been talking to some Christian, who's filled your head with all this flowery nonsense."

"I have not been talking to Christians! As if that is not obvious!"

"Swear?"

"Of course I swear!" said the sister, in her deepest voice. She was blushing furiously, though Rolf could not see it. She went on. "And, what's more, speaking as a Viking, I hate flowers! Flowers of all colours and description! Never again will I compare the gods to pretty flowers. How silly of me. How silly!"

"That's better," said the eldest. "And I will agree with you that this is an urgent matter. I've been saying that the whole time."

Rolf turned his head ever so slowly and peeked over at his captors. In the glint of the fire, and despite his own groggy vision, he could see that they were not much more than children themselves. Some of them looked to be his own age, and the eldest was clearly only a few years older than him.

And then Rolf felt the itch against his ear again. And then he finally realized what was causing it.

8

The Multi-Syllabic Giant

RAT-A-TASK had clutched frantically to the inside of Rolf's shirt while the giant was falling endlessly through the air and plunging into the water. They went down so deep that Rat-A-Task thought he might drown. And then they surfaced again, much to his relief. But the relief was short-lived. Rolf hit the rock and the squirrel saw that he was unconscious and rolling forward onto his chest, face down, in the water. Rat-A-Task scurried around to the back of Rolf's collar and then, realizing that the boy was in grave danger of drowning, sunk his teeth into his ear to try and revive him. Rolf didn't even flinch. Rat-A-Task believed again that his little life was over. But then the sons of Erik Blood-Axe waded into the river, hand clasping hand, until their human chain reached the giant. And they dragged him out, together with his hidden squirrel.

And then, as the boys dragged the unconscious giant over to their camp, Rat-A-Task, whom the morning light had revealed to have fur coloured an orangey kind of red, had skittered up into the shaggy locks of Rolf's red hair and held for dear life onto the boy's right ear. Camouflaged, as it were. Not to mention hidden by the ear, which was very big, even for a giant. There he clung, chattering softly, "Wake up, Rolf, wake up. Wake up, Rolf."

Until, to the squirrel's gigantic relief, Rolf finally woke up.

"Listen to me," the squirrel said. "Listen carefully. You're going to have to talk to these people. They're dangerous people and cannot be reckoned with lightly. But they can be reckoned with, by such a mind as mine. In a moment, I'm going to ask you to speak. I'm going to ask you to proclaim certain ideas in a commanding voice. Have you got a problem with that? DON'T say anything. I'm going to ask you—and this is the most crucial point—to speak more than one word at a time. I suspect you're capable of it. I suspect you only refrain out of shyness. Am I correct? DON'T say anything. You'll prove your understanding simply by repeating after me when the time comes."

Rolf did understand, though he was worried about whether it was wise to speak to an obviously hostile group of people. But he was not about to argue, and anyway he was incapable of it, and anyway he was tied up, and anyway the squirrel pressed on.

"So here's the first sentence," said Rat. "Are you ready? DON'T say anything. Here it comes: 'Behind us stands the Tree of the World!' Shout it!"

"Behind!" shouted Rolf, without thinking. Though he was wet and aching, he still felt ready to speak. "Behind!" he shouted again, to be sure he'd said it. And then he realized that he had, and then said it again. And then he realized it was just one word he'd said, and there was no reason to believe he might say anymore. And then he saw the seven siblings turn and look at him. This increased the pressure on him to speak correctly the many words he'd been given to say. But what if they came out in the wrong order?

"Behind!" he said again, a fourth time. The Haralds were staring at him now. He wanted to point above his head, in the direction of what he thought was the waterfall. But he was tightly bound. The ropes burned the skin around his wrists. He looked at the Haralds and tried to form his features into a frown. No: worse than a frown. A glower. But that didn't work. He listened for the squirrel, but the squirrel said nothing, waiting patiently (presumably with his little paws crossed like fingers, his eyes shut tight) for Rolf to work his way through the sentence he'd given him.

Rolf was, for the moment, on his own. So then, what would work? He thought of the bump on his head and the ache where his ear had been bitten. He thought of the waterfall he could not see but was presumably behind him. He thought of how he'd climbed the rock face and pulled himself up onto the slippery plateau. He thought of the cave opening and the patch of sun. He thought of the tree. The tree in all its beauty. And little Idun, who would be protected along with all the other dwellers there. And then he opened his mouth again.

"The Tree of the World!" he said.

"That's right, that's right," said the squirrel. "The Tree of the World. Say it again, say it again."

"The Tree of the World," said Rolf, without shouting.

And he saw the expressions on the faces of the Haralds change. They lost their hard composure, at least for a moment, and gazed up at the waterfall. It would seem that they, like the squirrel, had been told stories of the Tree of the World, even if they had never seen it. It seemed, by the expressions on their faces, they had almost stopped believing in it. Belief in such a tree is at the very centre of what it is to be a Viking. They called it *Yggðrasil*, which is a word I can't even pronounce, much less spell. Some of them even called it *askr Yggðrasil*, with many strong arguments as to why it should be called that and not simply *Yggðrasil*. But I'm not going to get into that.

Still, despite being Vikings, and despite looking upward for a long open-mouthed moment, the Haralds turned back toward the tied-up and tongue-tied giant with their skepticism as strong as ever. Because of course there wasn't anything up on the face of that cliff that looked like a tree, much less a Tree of the World.

But Rolf's words had accomplished something. If only for a moment. He'd seen it. It gave him confidence to go on.

"Hidden," he said. "Hidden there. Hidden." And then, though the squirrel was waiting to see what the Haralds would say, Rolf went on. Spoke a few words he made up in his head. All by himself.

"The Tree of the World is still young," he said, barely believing he was speaking. "And parts of it are very small and delicate. It's hidden from our sight, behind that cliff. Behind that waterfall. It's full of living things. And it has living leaves clinging to it, that whisper in your ear. It is a wonder. And it holds up everything. And it needs protecting."

Rolf had said much, by anybody's standards. Rat-A-Task hung dumbstruck by his ear. The Haralds stood open-mouthed and looked at him. Finally, the eldest spoke.

"It's true," he said. "If there is indeed a Tree of the World standing behind the face of the mountain, if indeed it does exist, then such a precious place might indeed require protecting. I don't know, however, why a giant would give us this information, considering that giants are malevolent beings."

"Why?" asked Rolf, who had never heard the stories heretofore reported about giants demanding daughters or riches. The squirrel starting chittering by his ear again, but Rolf wasn't paying attention. "Why do you say that giants are mal—malel—maloleo—"

"It's just their prejudice," whispered the squirrel. "I'll explain later. Tell them you're here to protect the tree!"

"I am here to protect the tree!" shouted Rolf, who knew it was true.

"Tell us then, giant," declaimed the eldest. "If you are here to protect the Tree of the World, from what does it need protecting?"

"From what? . . ."

Of course, Rolf did not know himself.

"It is not the first time this tree has grown, you know," said the squirrel. "Tell them that, and see how they respond."

"It is not the first time this tree has grown," repeated Rolf, who then went on. "Tell them *oops*." He had finished repeating the phrase and then started the statement that was meant for him alone. Hrrmph. So then he stopped and hoped no one noticed and waited patiently for the squirrel to go on.

"Deep in the earth," the squirrel dictated, "below its crust—below this part of the earth that we call the Earth itself—in another realm, there is another tree, an enormous tree. Dead. Fallen beside where the new one is growing. Evidence that it has grown before and been cut down."

"From where do you have this knowledge?" asked the eldest to Rolf, who had repeated every word.

Rolf cleared his throat as he waited for the squirrel to think of what to say. This conversation was getting very complicated for a boy who had only just begun to speak out loud in complex sentences. He wished that he could just say, "I was told all this by Rat-A-Task, the squirrel. His mother told him. She spoke a language called Chkkt. He's right here, clinging to my ear, and can tell you all about it."

He did not say this though. Instead, he repeated what the squirrel finally whispered to him.

"I should not tell you," he said, "because it's doubtful you'll believe me."

"If you do not tell us," said the boy hotly, "then we will believe exactly nothing at all, not that there is any living tree there now, nor that there is a dead one beside it."

"It was a Dreki who told me," said the squirrel finally. "Curled down at the bottom of the tree, around its roots. He knows how to protect it. I'm following his instructions."

Rolf repeated these words, wondering whether his listeners would be as shocked as he had been by the mention of the Dreki.

"A Dreki?" shouted the eldest impatiently. "That's even harder to believe than you seeing the Tree of the World! You, giant, are full of lies. No one has seen a Dreki for hundreds of years! Only their bones buried in the ground and scattered about! It's far from certain that there's ever even been such a thing!"

Rolf felt so indignant at being called a liar that he was happy to repeat the next volley from the squirrel.

"How can you believe in gods and giants but not Drekis?" he asked.

"How can we not believe in giants, when there is one right here before us?"

"It's true," said Rolf, still following the squirrel's lead. "You may not have seen a Dreki. But, as certain as I am bound here before you, I have. I have seen a Dreki with my own two eyes!"

(Rolf found this last somewhat odd to say, since he had not, in fact, seen a Dreki with his own two eyes.)

"You have, have you?" asked the eldest.

"Yes, I have seen a Dreki: that great reservoir of knowledge, speaker of the future as well as the past, more scholarly even than the humble little squirrel—"

"Who said squirrels were scholarly!" shouted the eldest. "Stop talking nonsense!"

This statement brought the conversation to an abrupt halt, Rat-A-Task remaining silent for a long time—several crucial seconds—as he contemplated how to correct such callous ignorance.

"Do not torment me with your lack of knowledge," he said finally, and then waited for Rolf to repeat before going on. "You make me lose hope. The task I wish to give you is difficult enough! But if you lack the wisdom to learn from those who are smarter than you, even if they appear to be weak and tiny creatures, then you will surely fail!"

The eldest of the Haralds had flushed almost to the colour of the fire burning behind him. Finally he mustered: "Laying aside for a moment the absurd proposition that *you* are going to give *us* a task, I will say I may be young, but I am far from ignorant. I may know little about squirrels, but I can still be trusted with a task if I judge it worthy. And so can my brothers." He stopped and composed himself, and then went on. "I am willing to believe you saw a Dreki. I am willing to believe even that there lies a dead tree beside the living. But all my belief rests on one crucial thing I must see with my own eyes."

"The tree," said Rolf.

"Indeed," said the eldest. "The Tree of the World. I must climb up and see it and then we will decide if you have anything else worth saying."

And then the second eldest, the sister, spoke up. "I have heard," she said, in her gruffest voice, "that giants are great lovers of beauty. Perhaps, if the tree really exists, this one wishes to protect it for the sake of its beauty."

"That is true!" shouted Rolf, surprising everyone with his fervor before the squirrel had a chance to coach him. "I would lay down my life in defence of the Tree of the World!"

And the squirrel, who knew that he himself would never be able to lay down his life for anything, was glad he had chosen his giant so well.

"Very well," said the eldest. "But I must see this tree."

The matter was discussed and it was decided that Rolf would be untied and that he would then take the two eldest siblings and climb up the cliff. Each of them would cling to a shoulder and hold a blade to Rolf's throat, one on each side, so that he would not be able to act against them.

"What if the climb gets bumpy?" asked Rolf.

"I trust you'll manage to keep it smooth," said the eldest.

"It will only be the second time I've ever done it," said Rolf. "And I slipped the first time on the way down."

It was true. None of the Haralds would ever forget the cry they had heard from above, and then the sight of the giant falling from that high, high place into the middle of the foaming river. It gave them pause to think of two of their numbers put at such precarious risk.

"Very well," said the eldest. "I will go alone. And I will not use my blade if you swear to do your best to return me safely."

"I swear," said Rolf.

And so they untied Rolf, and the eldest climbed onto his back even as Rat disappeared into his collar. Rolf walked over to the cliff wall and began his ascent. He knew he was being watched by many pairs of eyes, and it made him self-conscious. But also, strangely, it seemed to give him strength and sureness with his grip against the crevices and rocks along the face.

It took the better part of an hour to get to the top. Finally, Rolf pulled himself up onto the ledge and waited there while the eldest son slipped off his back and climbed by himself through the crevice and down into the tree. Rolf did not wish to look himself, since he feared that, if he did, he would be unable to tear himself away.

Eventually, the eldest returned to the ledge. Rolf looked into his eyes and knew that the boy had just visited the most beautiful place in the world. And the eldest looked back at Rolf and knew that he had seen such a place too. They still did not trust each other — not by any means — but they understood one aspect of one another, where resided an appreciation for the Tree of the World. And they understood too that this made them allies in its defence.

"What do you want us to do?" asked the eldest Harald.

"I will tell you when we return to the riverbank," said Rolf.

"Very well."

And so they climbed back down. And the other sons and daughters of Erik Blood-Axe strained their necks to watch them as they came. And then they sat and rubbed their necks as Rolf (and Rat-A-Task) instructed them to set out on a journey in search of all the giants in the land. To approach each of them and appeal to their better natures. To tell them how they were destined to come and see the most beautiful thing in the world, how they were destined to protect it. How nobody could protect the Tree of the World better than an army of giants.

"If you explain it to them in this way," said Rolf, "there is no question but that they will come."

All the other Haralds looked to the eldest to see if they should trust this giant's words. The eldest turned to them and nodded.

"It's true," he said. "I've seen how much this giant loves that tree. I do believe, if the rest are like him and if we explain it this way, they will come."

So the seven sons of Erik Blood-Axe made their pledge and set off to fulfill their task, promising to be back inside of a week with a throng of Norse giants.

"Or else," said the eldest, "we will cross to Denmark and find them there!"

As they watched them go, Rolf asked Rat-A-Task what they were going to do while they waited.

"I don't know about you," said the squirrel, "but I have a nest to build, in that tree. The biggest drey this winter world has ever seen!"

"What is a drey?" asked Rolf.

"You'll see," said the squirrel. "Come on."

And before the sun had hit the centre of the sky, Rolf and the squirrel had reached the slippery plateau of the cliff and slipped through the crevice that brought them down into the embrace of the Tree of the World. Rat scurried off to plan the architecture of his drey in the tree's safe embrace, while Rolf climbed down in search of the tiny leaf named Idun who had never been far from his thoughts.

9

Return of The Beaky

THE SONS OF ERIK BLOOD-AXE had been travelling for several hours when, just as the sun was setting somewhere behind the clouds, they encountered The Beaky, who didn't notice their approach because he was far too preoccupied with trying to recapture his horse.

Or rather, first they encountered the horse, standing in the half light among the trees, nickering and blowing and nervous. Tied to its cloth saddle was a pair of dangling snowshoes. Peering closely, one might have seen a few old falcon feathers still caught among the ties. And then, just a little way beyond, was The Beaky himself, trying unsuccessfully to stalk his mount. The Beaky had in fact been following his horse for miles, through the darkness and the day and again

81

the growing darkness. The horse would stop to graze and allow his master to get within ten paces before he calmly cantered over another hill or through another patch of woods, forcing the poor Beaky to start his stalking all over again.

Do you remember how, in the book known as *The Feathered Cloak*, the blindfolded and captive Morton decided to fight back, escape from his guards, and run skittering into the woods? Bikki Number Four had been knocked off his horse—a fine gelding named Nicker—and it had run away. Believe it or not, that took place only a few days ago, not long before the poor, poor Bikki Number Four had been transformed, through an act of the heart, into the far more sympathetic and lovable Beaky, who dressed up as a bird out of a wish to emulate that same honourable old falcon who had been so badly mistreated and who had stood by a young girl in battle, won the day, and died.

But just because The Beaky had become a kinder person did not mean his life was going to get any easier. It did not mean, in other words, that it was going to be any easier for him to catch a horse than it had been for him to catch a falcon.

But he wanted his horse back. Nicker was the only creature he'd ever been allowed to be kind to, at least while labouring under the yoke of Erik Blood-Axe. And so the gelding was essentially his best and only friend. Which made it particularly heartbreaking for The Beaky to see how much the horse enjoyed avoiding him.

It must be said, though, that, to a horse, the sight of a man dressed like a bird is probably deeply unsettling. It takes some getting used to. The Beaky understood this, even if he was exhausted and grumbly, and so he endured his trial with patience, hoping that it would eventually come to an end.

And so here he was, in all his black-clad and birdlike glory. The Haralds stood among the trees and watched, somewhat transfixed, as The Beaky hopped through the snow, one foot and then the other, then the other. They wondered for a moment if he was a berserker—one of those famous mad warriors who could fight entire battalions with reckless zeal. But this birdlike man looked far too fragile to be a berserker. His arms were like skinny branches, popping out at odd angles. His knees were as knobby as pine cones. The Haralds wondered too whether he wasn't trying, absurdly, to dress up like one of Odin's ravens—those mythical messengers who caw their way through the damp, snow-clad landscape, reminding people everywhere how there had once been a one-eyed god watching over everything.

The eldest Harald cleared his throat loudly, catching the attention of the black-clad Beaky and causing him to spin in the snow and stand practically at attention, showing all the skills of a former courtier to the king, instantly prepared with a bow, a greeting, and an explanation.

"I am The Beaky," said The Beaky. "I am a bird and

I have misplaced my horse. I am pleased to make your acquaintance."

"You are most certainly not a bird," countered the eldest Harald bluntly, "and I will kill you before asking you to refrain from saying anything so ridiculous again. You are not a bird, but rather the most pathetic human creature I have ever seen. Someone pretending to be something he is not."

The Beaky blushed and then paled and then blushed again. He'd found himself in this kind of situation before, specifically when Erik Blood-Axe had first mocked him as he delivered news that a thief of a girl and a washed-up old hunting hawk had been protected by powerful women warriors with wings. He was beginning to get used to it. He stood up to his full height and stuck out his chin in an attempt to convey courage and pride. "I could not help but hear your contempt, though you may have been trying to hide it," he said, trying to give the benefit of the doubt.

"I was not trying to hide it," corrected the Harald.

"Be that as it may, I know that tone well, from my former days with the equally contemptuous Erik Blood-Axe."

"We are familiar with the king whose name you sully. He is our father."

"Well . . . ," said The Beaky. "That's . . ." He was speechless. He knew Erik had sons, but it was the kind of information about Erik that tended to slip one's mind, since these children had been raised far away from the centre of power, so as not to weaken their father through the gradual accumulation of paternal tenderness. Erik was always vigilant about such things.

Now The Beaky was being presented with the seven children of his former employer and sovereign. He didn't know whether to be terrified or touched.

"It is an honour," he said, bowing low, "to meet the brave sons of the former king." And for the sentimental Beaky, indeed it was. Despite everything that had happened to him, he still felt the old tug of loyalty.

"Wait a moment," said the eldest, while the others stood and laughed. "I know who you are. You're one of the Bikki. Have you not pledged a life of allegiance to our father? Why have you not gone with him on his journey across the sea?"

"He has dismissed me," replied The Beaky, humbly.

"Why?"

The Beaky shrugged and said nothing. He did not want to say anything against the father in front of the children. So the eldest Harald ventured his own conclusion.

"Because of your incompetence."

"There is no other reason, I suppose," said The Beaky. "Though it should perhaps be added that I do not regret my incompetence in this case—the escape, from my charge, of a sadly mistreated hunting hawk."

"You!" said the eldest, realizing. "You were the bungler of the old falcon. I was told of your errors. If it weren't for your errors and an imposter Valkyrie, my father would still be king."

The seven sons took a step closer to The Beaky. Seven steps all together.

"You grant me more credit than I deserve," said the former Bikki Number Four, taking a single step back to counter their seven. "But how could you ever call our renowned Freya the falcon-catcher an impostor?"

"For following the edicts of a Christian king!" shouted the eldest, taking, with his brothers, another step.

"A good king, rather," corrected The Beaky, moving slowly back. "I was there, and I happen to know King Haakon's beliefs were not as important as the idea of being a good steward of his people."

The eyes of all the Haralds flashed so brightly that the sun seemed to emerge from behind the clouds. "You were present on the Field of Snorre and still you would speak against our father?"

They were getting very close to him now.

"I do believe I am going to be hurt," said The Beaky, bleakly but calmly, backed against a tree.

But then suddenly another man was there. A stranger. He seemed to have appeared out of nowhere and was standing now between The Beaky and the seven outraged siblings. There was a large sword hanging from a scabbard in his belt, but the man's hands were clasped calmly behind his thickset back. And he wore the strangest helmet The Beaky had ever seen. The

Haralds had taken a step back, surprised, when they first saw him, but then they too saw his helmet and began to laugh.

"Stranger!" shouted the eldest. "You're standing in our way!"

"That I am," said the man.

"Don't you think you might have better things to do?"

"Like what, pray tell?"

"Like repairing your broken helmet?"

"My helmet is not broken," replied Egil, calmly. "It was made this way, if it's any of your business. My old dog made off with the other horn just before the hat was made. There was only one left, so I put it in the middle, where it would be better employed. Better, I think, than punishing the poor dog, who was only acting according to his nature. Anyway," he added, "the helmet and its horn proves to be a useful weapon when my hands are otherwise occupied, which might be the case today, since there are seven of you and only two of us."

The Beaky felt a throb of gratitude to be included in the stranger's calculations, swiftly followed by a stab of fear that he might be called upon to fight.

The seven Haralds, for their part, had hands on handshafts and swords half-drawn. Egil continued to stand calmly. The Beaky, behind him, looked from the poet to the Haralds and back again, and then he looked in the direction of his beloved horse, who was placidly nosing in the snow a few trees away and whom he quietly cursed for being responsible for this trouble.

"So then," said Egil, "enough pleasantries. Tell me, what is your business with this innocent fellow?"

"None of yours, stranger," replied the eldest, and the others echoed his statement.

"On the contrary," said Egil, "it *is* my business. I am a poet. As such, I'm always looking for matters of human import. And so I take an interest in my fellow men and their squabbles with one another. It gives me something to think about and something to write about. And, when it comes down to it, it gives me something to fight about."

At this, the Haralds drew their swords as one.

"Impressive," said Egil, smiling at their unison. "I wonder, was that luck? Or do you spend hours practising?" And then he laughed. "I'll bet you can't do it again!"

The siblings looked confused for a moment at this mockery of something they performed so proudly, and then they took a step forward. Egil continued to stand his ground. "I have a sword in my belt," he said, "along with a hidden dagger. Not to mention the aforementioned head-horn. But so what? I can fight you with my words alone. Watch me evoke a cloud-covered ax in poetry, and then smite you with it!"

With that word "smite," Egil took a single step forward, his hands still clasped behind his back. It was true, for a moment the Haralds thought they saw an ax of misty grey hovering in the air beside his left elbow, ready to be grasped and flung. Even The Beaky believed he saw it. The siblings took a step back before the seeming vision of the ax dissolved and they shook their heads.

"You are a witch," called the eldest.

"I am not," replied Egil. "Merely a wordsmith. Though it's true I fear no one more than that witch, your mother, Brunhilde. Yes, I know who you are. You are the sons of Erik Blood-Axe. And though I hate him and his witchling wife, those two who together drove me into exile, still I will not fight you. You are, after all, clearly just children."

(Forgive me, dear reader, for not mentioning Brunhilde before. The simple explanation is that I've always been terrified of her and try to think of her as little as possible. Be assured that she does indeed exist in this story, was present on the beach when the king was about to sail into exile, and is as mean as they come. But I'm going to stop talking about her now.)

"Ha!" shouted the eldest. "I have done more in my life than you could ever dream of! How could you, Egil the charlatan, Egil the magician, Egil the irritating, stuck on a small island in the ocean for many years, have come close to having the adventures I've had with Norway and Denmark and all of Europe at my feet!"

"Then you have heard of me," said Egil. "And you are boastful. It's not a good quality in a grown-up. You should work on that. It is not helpful, especially when you do not know how to properly address your opponent. I, for example, should be addressed by no other title than Poet. I am Egil the Poet."

And then the Haralds charged. It's true, I admit, they were brave, since they knew who this man was and how dangerous, and perhaps even how their fighting would not end well for them. But they knew he was an enemy to their father and so they felt they had no choice but to fight.

And then Egil took a step back and spoke his poetry. Ten or fifteen choice words that have never been recorded and will not be written here.

10

Egil Am I

THE BROTHERS AND SISTERS lay flat upon the ground, looking up through the trees at the sky. It occurred to many of them in that moment (in their own private individual ways) how rarely it was they looked up at the sky. It was true it was grey, but it was still something to see, especially since there were shapes to be perceived within the grey, and there was the sense of whether the clouds were hanging low or flying high, and whether they would swirl or rowl or bring sleet or snow, or just sit there like a sluggish mood.

And then they realized, pretty much as one, that they had somehow been knocked to the ground, and that their swords were laying beside them. They had never experienced anything like what they had just now and were still in shock.

The Beaky too was lying on his back in the snow behind the poet. He tried to be grateful—tried not to think about how the damp would seep through to his drawers and make him feel uncomfortable. But it was a challenge, as this was his least favourite thing in the world. The horse that he blamed for all his current troubles had cantered away a short distance, where he now stood blowing in The Beaky's direction, as if to say, "What are you waiting for? Let's get out of here!" But The Beaky knew he didn't mean it.

"It's true," said Egil, walking now among the fallen Haralds, "I owe my new capacity for powerful words to that father of yours, who exiled me and my family. It's true, I used to be more boastful than powerful with my words. It's true too I was a bit of a thief, at least from your father's point of view. A thief of time and ears, what with me speaking my terrible verses. Since I have your attention, let me give you an example of the sort of thing your forebears had to endure."

And then, much to The Beaky's surprise, Egil lowered his chin, deepened his voice by half an octave, and created the distinct impression of a man who took himself very seriously. Egil even stood up on the tips of his toes, as if he thought he would be seen better that way, and became, very suddenly, an earnest, idealistic, and terrible young poet.

And with a Final Great Heave of Breath, HE Died.
     NEVER to rise again from the bed.
And the people GRIEVED their loss, it was evening
     and none returned to his home:
Their king was DEAD, and the people dropped to the
     ground where they stood, lay through the night on
     the floors of the Royal Rooms . . .

They were, presumably, the last words of a very long tribute to Erik's father, Harald Finehair. The Beaky found that his eyelids were beginning to droop as Egil went on.

Hundreds of them, SIDE by SIDE, bearing silently
     together the WEIGHT of their LOSS,
Wrapped in blankets, silent weeping; here for a pillow a
     shoulder, there for some comfort a hand.
Hundreds of them, I have said it before, they SHARED
     the WORK of GRIEF . . .

Struggling to keep alert and polite, The Beaky saw that the poet's words were having a similar effect on the sons and daughters of Erik Blood-Axe, all of whom were lying on the ground with eyes closed and mouths open as Egil strolled among them.

SILENT in the palace, CENTRE of their CITY so
     SILENT, so DARK: so DARK and SILENT
That a RUTHLESS army FAILED to see them,

MARAUDERS MARCHING SOUTH through
WILD LANDS in search of CONQUEST, saw
them not and went on marching,
SOUTH and to the SEA.
They DREW their WEAPONS, they fought the SEA
and LOST, but that's another story.
Here a GREAT DEAD KING saves his people through
the GREATNESS of his loss: the GREATNESS of
their GRIEF. That is the end of my tale.

And then, just as abruptly, Egil changed back again, waking the seven Haralds and The Beaky too.

"Do you understand how bad that was?" the poet asked. "Or shall I speak some more?"

He raised his hand before anyone had a chance to object. "No, I think you get the idea. It was difficult for people to listen to me in those days, especially since I always had a bit of a temper. If anyone fell asleep I used to tiptoe up to them, raise my sword and chop off an ear or two! Just kidding. I only did it once. Well, maybe twice."

Egil distracted himself for a moment, counting on his fingers before dropping the notion and going on. "Still, what do you expect? I was a young man! I didn't know any better! And it takes an awfully long time to make something short! All I ever wanted in those days was the respect of the king."

He paused and took stock of his listeners. Everyone was paying strict attention to him, as if they all thought they were going to get their ears cut off too. He sighed, annoyed by something, The Beaky could not tell what, and then went on.

"Respect from the king, however, was not forthcoming. I had always striven to deliver my verses within earshot of him, so that he might raise me up to the realm of court poet or some such grand position. You can imagine what a burden that must have been for the man. Naturally, he banished me. How could he not?

"Fine, you might say. Good! I deserved banishment, due to my pride and my bad verses. But once in Iceland, which is as far away as you children can imagine —no matter what you might say about Europe being at your feet—I saw my wife die, along with my children and my poor father, and even the old dog that I spoke of before. All were engulfed in a river of fire that flowed from the earth and covered acre after acre of land.

"When I first saw it—since I had been away from home when it happened, trying to map that gods-forsaken island—I stood at the edge of the sea of bubbling rock and cried out with such grief, with such a desire for my wife to hear me, even if she was buried beneath a league of stone, that the rock rolled back and I discovered I had a new power I did not need: The power to push and hurl and dig with my words alone."

Egil went down on one knee. For a moment he seemed overcome with emotion, as if a torrent was about to burst from his eyes and he had to struggle to push it back. And then he continued.

"I would never have gone to that wretched place, were it not for your father. The lava took away everything I have ever loved, along with my penchant for terrible poetry. It left me with those more powerful ways of wording you witnessed earlier. So what, I say. Who cares? What's the difference between bad verses and good verses? Who cares? I'm not even sure I want to live. Could I have saved my family if I had been with them when the fire came? That's the only important question, and I will never know the answer. Could I have offered them courage and comfort even if we were all about to die together? This too I don't know how to answer. But I can stop such puny aggression as this you've given me here. Drawn swords. Phooey. If you want to fight me, choose better words. Nothing else will help you. So you must thank your father for me, when you see him again, for giving me this small meaningless victory over you, here in the land of my versing's birth."

The Haralds still lay in the snow and did not move.

Egil stood up again. "Tell me now," he continued, "since I proved by the force of word and arm that all this is indeed of some concern to me, what is your business with this fellow behind me? It must be important, by the way you were harrying him."

"Our business," said the eldest, "is to admonish him for leaving our father's service."

Egil turned to The Beaky, addressing him for the first time in a friendly tone. "Did you leave the service of Erik Blood-Axe?" he asked.

"He dismissed me and sentenced me to death," shrugged The Beaky.

Egil looked back significantly at the eldest Harald, still lying on the ground.

"All right then," said the eldest, sounding more and more like a child. "We have no business with him. But you have to let us go, since we do have business to attend to, as dire as anything you could imagine!"

"I can imagine a great deal," said Egil. "Tell me what it is and perhaps I'll let you go about it."

So the sons of Erik Blood-Axe told the single-horned stranger what had taken place at the waterfall. They all spoke up, feeling a little like children, which was how this man made them feel.

They told Egil about the giant who fell from the top of the cliff, whom they captured, and who had won them over with his words about the wonders of the newly growing Tree of the World—a tree that was coming up to cradle the whole of the earth in its strong and beautiful branches, as it did many generations before, and provide compelling evidence for the return of the gods, something they wished for more than anything else.

They told him too about the Dreki—a creature renowned for its certain knowledge of the future—and how this giant had claimed to have seen one deep inside, down at the bottom of the tree, its root. And how the Dreki had advised the giant that the tree was in danger and required an army of giants to protect it. And how the Haralds themselves had been given the task of rounding up these giants.

Egil stood and listened to this melodramatic tale, wrinkling his nose, pulling off his helmet, and contemplating the horn while running a hand absently through his damp hair. He could not help wondering whether these—after all—children were merely exercising their childish right to imagine a world that did not exist anymore, if it ever had.

"How do you justify trusting a giant?" he finally asked.

"Two reasons," said the eldest. "He spoke well of the beauty of the tree."

"Could he not have been lying?" asked Egil.

"He was a child. He did not seem to know how to dissemble."

"The world is rarely as it seems," said Egil. "Though I can see how that would make an impression. What is your second reason?"

"He showed it to me," said Harald. "And returned me to the ground, unharmed."

"He showed you the Tree of the World?"

The Haralds all nodded.

"And the Dreki?" asked Egil.

They admitted that none of them had seen the Dreki.

"It would have been a long journey down the tree and into the belly of the earth," explained the eldest.

"I see," said Egil. "You were lazy."

"I was not!" shouted the eldest. "We merely wanted to get on with it!"

"In a hurry to start your adventures. But if this giant was just a child, where did he get the authority to send you on a mission?"

"As I said before, he spoke well."

"Was somebody instructing him?"

The Haralds looked at each other and shrugged. "He fell from the sky. He was completely alone."

Egil stood quietly for a few moments, deep in thought, the Haralds all waiting for him to speak again.

For his part, The Beaky wondered over all this talk about a wise and eloquent child giant. The Beaky had only ever met one giant and it just so happened that he was a child. Rolf the Ranger, brother of Freya the Bold. But Rolf was a shy boy who rarely spoke a word. Perhaps here indeed was proof of other giants in the world.

"Hmmm," said Egil finally. "All right then. I've heard enough. Be on your way."

The eldest hesitated.

"So you sanction the task?" he finally asked.

Egil realized how truly childlike they were, so swiftly had they invested him with authority. "What is it to me," he asked, "how you spend your time?"

"Advise us!" shouted the eldest Harald, in his most commanding voice. Egil frowned for a moment, then laughed and nodded his head.

"Very well," he said. "If you're going to embark on such a journey, don't you think it would be better to split up? You'll gather more giants that way. I think too that you would waste less time if you were more polite to those whose appearance you do not understand. Like, for example, this black-clad birdlike fellow here behind me. That's all the advice you're going to get from me, and I'll wager it's all you need. Off you go then. Go collect your giants."

And then, as the Haralds turned to go, Egil felt a change of mood and spoke again, not so friendly this time.

"Be warned, however," he called after them. "When the times comes, your giants may have to contend with me. Nobody can be certain of an ally in me; nobody! Especially not the sons of Erik Blood-Axe!"

Egil watched as the Haralds marched off in seven different directions, dispirited after his final words. And then he turned to The Beaky.

"So," he said, brightly now, his mood changing again in a flicker. "How would you like to go see a Dreki?"

"I would not," said The Beaky, who was thankful to this stranger but had no great interest in sharing such an adventure. His simple plan was to retrieve his horse and set off into the wilderness in search of his mother, whom he had not seen in many years.

"But you owe me," said Egil, still friendly.

"That I do," admitted The Beaky, swallowing hard.

"Such a debt would normally be paid in battle. I can guarantee, however, that if you come with me, I will protect you from all such battles, since you were clearly not made to fight."

"I see," said the blushing Beaky, remembering his warrior training with the Bikki. Still, he was content to be known as a non-fighter.

"And besides, I could use the company. Tell me, have you no interest at all in seeing a thing that has a name like the Tree of the World? Of course, I can't guarantee that you won't be disappointed, but if you're not, it will be a sight! Don't you agree?"

And then he walked over and clapped The Beaky on the shoulder, like a long-lost uncle.

"Here," he said. "How about I help you get your horse?"

Two human figures move easily through the landscape, sitting on top of their horses. One of them has a single horn on his head, which looks from a distance like an eye, bugging out and scanning the landscape. The other, dressed all in black, looks, it's true, more like a raven than a hawk. If someone were to see the two of them, riding through the forests and snow-clad meadows, he might take them for something out of an old story, almost forgotten, about a one-eyed wanderer and his raven companion—a god in fact, different in kind from all the other gods of the world because he was mortal. Still wise, though. It was possible for Odin to be both mortal and wise.

11

The Winter Drey

ROLF WANTED to know how he could help.

"You just have to know," said the squirrel. "You just have to have a feel for what twig will be right. Or what dried leaf or bit of wool. Or if a half an acorn shell will fit just so at the corner of the wall. Even an old bone, if you use it respectfully enough. You just have to know."

And the squirrel told him what it would feel like in there.

"When I sleep, I will hear the rustling of someone above me and someone below me. And all around I will hear the scampering through the hollows and the branches of the tree."

"Will there be room enough for me?" asked Rolf.

"My boy, my boy," said the squirrel, "look around you.

If there's one thing we have a great deal of, here in this tree, it is room. And this will be the largest squirrel drey that ever was made. Guest rooms for all the squirrels that will surely want to visit."

"But I am not a squirrel," said Rolf.

"You are a giant," said the squirrel. "And the giants are destined to be the protectors of the Tree of the World. As such, they are automatically protectors of the squirrels who live there. So giants will always be honoured guests in our drey."

Rolf was happy with the idea that he was going to be a protector, so he threw himself into the task of bringing materials to the squirrel. Rat-A-Task took only a small fraction of what he brought, but Rolf didn't care. He was learning all about the architecture of the nest. Maybe, once he had mastered the squirrel system, he'd be able to move to that of birds and butterflies with their cocoons, and so become the most renowned authority on nest architecture in all the animal, entomological, and mythical kingdoms. And it was just like walking in the woods, as he foraged. It gave him a task to perform as he trembled with love for this place, among the leaves and branches and all along the trunk.

This was when Rat finally told him the stories of the animosities between the giants and the gods, though Rolf did not like these stories at all.

"So, gods think giants are stupid?" he asked.

"They consider themselves to be superior, yes,"

said the squirrel.

"Well," said Rolf, feeling indignant. "They can think what they like. I'm not even sure they exist."

"Of course they exist," said Rat. "What do you think your sister is?"

"My sister? What does she have to do with anything?"

"The goddess Freyja is known for her feathered cloak," said Rat. "Sound familiar?"

Rolf could not believe what he had just heard. It did not make any sense. His sister had not always had a feathered cloak. She'd just acquired it the other day—and not because she was a goddess either, but rather because she was a brave little girl who was trying to help out her friend Morton the falcon.

Rolf explained all this to the squirrel.

"So?" replied Rat, simply. "Things change."

Rolf wasn't sure he wanted things to change as much as all that.

"So . . . ," he said, "you're saying my sister is—"

"A goddess, yes," said the squirrel. "But I thought you knew that. Why do you think you had to leave her behind?"

Rolf felt indignant again. "I'm not sure why I had to leave her behind. All I know is I was told I had to leave her behind. You told me."

"She is a goddess," said the squirrel, patiently. "And you are a giant. Destined to be enemies. Your father must have known that too. If he did not tell you any of those stories, it was probably because he didn't want to upset you."

"Hrumph," said Rolf, who was feeling more and more upset. "You think my sister thinks I'm stupid?"

"I know it," said Rat. "The best thing you can do is forget about her."

"What?" Rolf was shocked. He had never heard more terrible words. Forget about his sister? Rolf could never. He fell silent and climbed away from this upsetting conversation. He wanted to go find Idun and talk to her, calm her nervous fluttering, and so soothe his own tormented heart.

But, as he climbed, he wondered. Did his sister really think he was stupid? Like a stupid, clumsy giant? It was true that she called him an oaf. But what if she could see him now? So gentle with his friends, a squirrel and a leaf? Not clumsy at all. Not stupid.

"You seem sad!" cried Idun, in her quiet voice, as he arrived.

"Not anymore," said Rolf. "Since I'm with you."

"I'm happy with you too!" Idun called.

There was no better feeling in the world than when he cupped this leaf in his palm, careful not to tug her away from the twig that held her to the tree. She would shiver and he would soothe her and then, in a moment, it would seem like the breeze would grow still and Idun's fluttering would stop.

"Ahh," she said. "Now I can rest for a moment. So busy I am, feeling the hum of the world. It's so hard to sit still."

"Sit still," Rolf said. "I'll hold you. I'll keep the hum of the world at bay."

And so she rested. And Rolf sat and felt like he had some value. That, even if he was not small and delicate himself, he knew how to protect the delicacy of the world. Its beauty. Idun's beauty, as rare as Freya's wings.

If Freya did think he was stupid, and since she could not see him here, then her thinking had not changed, despite the fact that Rolf himself had changed so much. Wherever she was, she still thought he was stupid, even now, when he felt he'd become smart. It hurt him right in the centre of his heart. Between his happiness holding Idun and his sadness thinking about Freya, Rolf had never felt so confused. He wondered whether this was what it was to be grown up.

"I just want a friend," said Rolf.

"I am your friend!" cried Idun. "I am your friend forever!"

"Promise?"

"I promise!"

"I'm your friend forever too," said Rolf.

Perhaps this leaf did not have the wisdom of Freya's friend Morton. After all, she was just a leaf. But she still seemed to teach him things he hadn't known before. Mostly things about his own capacity for feelings and thoughts and words. Though she also taught him that he should not be afraid to bring old leaves to Rat for the drey. She assured him that leaves, once they reached the end of their lives, were happy to be used for warmth and comfort. They liked the idea that their usefulness went on even after they were spent.

Rolf had once thought the squirrel would be like a Morton for him. A wise friend. But Rat-A-Task was mostly for himself. And the more Rolf thought about it, the more he believed this leaf was the true precious friend he sought.

Considering these things, he always surprised himself with his own depth of feeling as well as his sudden capacity for eloquence. "Eloquence must come from feeling," he thought. "It must be the way that feelings can come out. Is that why I talk now and I did not before?"

He wondered whether that meant he did not have such feelings for his sister and his father. No, that couldn't be right. He had loved them. He loved them still. But he'd never known how to express his love. And so he'd stumbled and been clumsy.

"That's why I was clumsy," he realized. "And why I'm clumsy no longer. Words have taken my clumsiness away."

And then he returned to the task of gathering moss and twigs for Rat-A-Task. And even, when he was very careful, the occasional wrinkly leaf.

As they worked, Rat-A-Task regaled Rolf with his own stories, which were always happy, cozy memories from the hours and days following his birth. Rolf liked these stories, he had to admit, as he handed Rat twigs and leaves and threads from his own sweater. Even if he knew Rat would have chittered them to anyone, he still liked them. They had no beginning and no end. Just like life in this tree.

"We used to bundle together," said Rat-A-Task. "I would see leaf, twig, eye, and a mother bigger than the moon, whose fur was summer and whose eyes were both day and night. My home. My mother and my home."

"Home," said Rolf. "Mother."

Rolf had a secret about his own mother. It was from long ago, the mute hours soon after he was born, and he recalled it only because his memory, like that of all giants, was strong. Rolf remembered his mother taking him into her arms. He remembered her pale strong arms, black hair, and bright black eyes. He remembered her saying, "You are the love of my life. If you can't find one then make one." And then he had felt her hold him close and then hold him out again and look at him and narrow her eyes. And then look closely at his ears. After that she had frowned and put him down into a crib. He'd watched her leave the room, which was as big and long as the world for him, and from then on he remembered her as someone who was first remote, and then no longer there at all.

He remembered too, some years later, when he first

learned that Freya, even though she was older, had no memory of their mother. He remembered wanting to share his story with her, thinking she might like to hear some proof of her existence in their lives. But he realized that he could not know for certain what Freya would think of his story.

Because Rolf knew—deep in his deepest Freya-loving heart—that he had been the cause of his mother leaving. And he still wondered whether that had been what his father had told Freya there on the stoop, on that night they had spoken, several days ago now. It's why he was so certain that Freya could abandon him, even though they had struggled side by side late in the day on the Field of Snorre, after a day and a night of shared adventure. That woman they had seen on the battlefield, sitting on her horse, resplendent wings resting across her shoulders—she, after all, had not even cast a glance in his direction.

This too was why Rolf liked to keep his ears covered, though he had long since lost his hat. He didn't know what was so strange about them, but it was enough to know they were strange, especially from a mother's point of view. And then, later, when he grew, he knew why. She had predicted somehow, looking at his ears, that he would grow and grow and grow, like when you look at the big paws of a puppy and you know he will soon be too big for your bed.

Rolf wondered now, with his handful of twigs and discarded bark, whether he should tell Rat-A-Task about all of this. The squirrel had told him about the traditional animosity between gods and giants, and he wondered whether that had something to do with his mother leaving. But if his mother hated giants so much, then how was it that she had given birth to one?

He tried to comfort himself with this question, even though he didn't have an answer. He tried in fact to turn the question into a statement: His mother gave birth to him, a giant. Therefore she loved him. She had left them for some other reason, and he had simply misunderstood.

Or maybe not.

Anyway, he was happy here. In the tree. At least sort of. At least for now. He found he didn't have to think about the problems and puzzles of his history very much at all.

As for Rat-A-Task, he did not notice Rolf's ups and downs of mood. He felt nothing but inspired as he built his winter drey in the Tree of the World. It was because he remembered his first nest so vividly—every wrinkle, every shadow of a twig across the faces of his family. He would remember that little nest for all the rest of his days. To him, it would always represent the summit of perfection and the pinnacle of safety. That's why he wanted to build it again, at a hundred times its former size. Because deep down inside, even with all his ambitions, he didn't ever feel safe.

12

To the Bottom of It

"THIS MUST BE THE PLACE," said Egil. They were standing by a river, near the foot of a high cliff. It had begun to snow, but evidence of the Haralds' camp was still visible. Another ten minutes and they might have passed it by. Egil jumped from his horse to survey the signs. "Look, here is the spot where the giant lay, and there are the ropes that were cut to set him free. The sign of a neglectful father: These wastrels should have untied them to use again. And look here—the ashes of a fire and seven seating spots where sat the seven sons of Erik Blood-Axe. It's funny," he mused. "I thought Erik had daughters too. Look here though: They had a meal. And here, of course . . . ," he stood up from the trampled snow and turned toward the spray, ". . . is the waterfall."

113

The Beaky looked at the flat expanse of stone, going straight up, smoothed by centuries of water. His knees quivered at the sight of it, causing his horse to bridle and nearly bolt.

"I think I should stay here and keep watch," he ventured, hoping such a task might be welcome.

Egil, through some miracle, nodded his head.

"Very generous of you," he said, as they both dismounted. "Very generous. Leave the interesting task for me. Not that I'm in a mood to be interested," he added, with his characteristic sudden shift of attitude. "But still. Much appreciated. Who knows what enemy could emerge from those woods as I climb. You'll be able to fight them off until I get to safety."

"Oh," said The Beaky, thinking better of his offer. But it was too late. Egil thumped the now frightened Beaky on the back and walked toward the cliff. The Beaky looked around, trying to distract himself from thinking of the lonesome terrors ahead. He saw, just on the other side of the river, a curious collection of crows having a party, knocking snow caps off the top of a tight scrum of tall, thin trees. Safe from all attack, they were laughing and flying in wobbly arcs up and out and down, and then back to the safety of the trees. The Beaky watched, all fear forgotten for the moment, and imagined how it would be to fly like that. He wondered too how he might get over to the other side of the river, being as he was (naturally) afraid of the water. There was not much The Beaky was not afraid of. This The Beaky knew now for sure. Still, if he could surmount his fear, perhaps it would be worth it. Perhaps there might be some loose feathers he could collect for his coat. Such trinkets might not turn him into a flier, but they would still represent flight and freedom, future and hope.

"Here," said Egil abruptly, pulling a horn off his belt and handing it back. "This is a hunting horn. If I haven't returned and the giants arrive, blow it as hard as you can."

"But—" said The Beaky.

"If they are friendly," continued Egil, "blow it twice. Only once if you are under attack. That's an old trick. If you're under attack, you only have time for one anyway. Twice means you can take a leisurely approach." He laughed at The Beaky's expression. "And don't worry. I will hear it and come. I have ears to hear this horn."

"But," said The Beaky, "how long are you going to be gone?"

"Not too long, you hope," said the poet, looking up again at the waterfall. "It's hard to tell how big it is in there. And then there's the matter of the Dreki. If you can tell me how long it takes to have a conversation with a Dreki, then maybe I can tell you how long I'll be gone. I've never seen a Dreki. I don't really believe they exist. What do you think?"

The Beaky shook his head, unsure whether it was a serious question. Egil clapped him again on his shoulder, making a loud thump with the flat of his gauntlet and nearly knocking The Beaky off his feet.

"I'll miss you, friend," he said. "Hope you're still here when I get back."

And then he shook the wet snow off his shoulders, turned, and walked resolutely toward the cliff, leaving The Beaky to drift with his eyes back to the grove of trees and wonder when he was going to get his next meal.

Egil was not the best climber. He always felt like his head was getting in the way. Reaching his arms up around that big jagged head was always a chore, especially when he found himself in a tight spot. And the single horned helmet didn't make things any easier. At one point, about halfway up, he slipped and, as he held there with a single hand, pictured the smiling face of his wife and thought about letting go. But it was against his nature to let go of anything, whether it be a piece of meat or a stone or a flea in his hair or himself. So he hoisted himself up to a safer position and went on.

When he got to the top and climbed into the hollow of the cliff, Egil did not bat an eye. He was a poet, it's true. But a poet who has seen his world destroyed does not wish to admit there is anything new under the sun and will not hold his breath when presented with the bright beauty of nature.

Now all he said, as he looked at the tree and then

up through the clouds and then down into the depths, was, "It's big all right."

And then he climbed in and down.

On the way, he saw bird nests, with pinkish-grey eggs sitting quietly inside them. He saw a woodpecker, though he'd heard it for awhile before it ascended, drilling, into his view. He saw the swish of a tail and looked up in time to see a red squirrel disappear around the trunk, on its way closer to the sun. Egil felt alone and almost happy. He wondered how many creatures had scurried away in advance of his passing. There was, after all, an infinity of nooks and crannies in which they could hide from view. He put his ear against the trunk and listened. Heard some tiny knocks and scufflings and whispers, but could not begin to make out their meaning.

He had to admit the tree was beautiful, with green leaves as wide as sails holding their own against the gales of the sea. But then, after he had climbed for hours, descending into the shadowy regions, he felt needles begin to prod him and called the tree a conifer. "This is no ordinary tree," he admitted at last.

But before he got down so far, while the sun was still sometimes in his eyes and other times the shade, while the leaves were still deciduous, he caught sight of a giant, sleeping in the crook of a bough, nestled against a smooth expanse of bark along the trunk. The giant's hands were cupped, as if he had fallen asleep while trying to scoop some water to his face. But then Egil saw that they were cradling a small branch with a single tiny leaf. When he saw that, he felt no doubt in his mind. "Here be the boy," he thought. "Eloquent defender of beauty. Motivator of Erik's sons." Egil thought the boy looked about nine years old. "I'd be surprised if he's ever really clapped his eyes on a Dreki," Egil determined. "I'd bet my last crown he hasn't."

The giant looked peaceful and Egil really didn't want to break the silence of this dappled afternoon. Still, he knew he needed to speak to the boy. "Hello," he called from a safe distance away. And then again, "Hello!"

Rolf woke up. For a moment he forgot where he was, and then he recalled Idun the leaf, cupped in his hands, and looked anxiously at her. She was content and still in the afternoon.

And then he realized that there was someone, just below him, about ten yards away across the trunk, calling hello in a gruff voice. He looked over and saw him. The poet. Egil. Rolf immediately tried to recall the poem from the tree trunk, he wanted to recite it—

Egil am I . . .
Lost to the . . . volcano . . .

(No, that wasn't it.)

Driven from Norway,
Now I return . . .

—but found he was, again, tongue-tied. Maybe, he thought, I am stupid after all, just like Rat says Freya thinks.

All this time he was staring at Egil, and when he finally spoke, the only thing he could say was, "You."

Egil was surprised. "Me?" he asked. "Do you know me, son?" The word "son" came out unintended. He had not meant to sound friendly, had not meant to sound like he was no threat. But it was too late for that. He sighed.

"Worth," said Rolf, trying. And again. "Worth." Thinking again of the poem's *only here can I finally know my worth*. In fact, Rolf felt exactly the same way.

"Hello there, then," said Egil, not understanding any of this from the single word *worth*. "Sorry to wake you. I was wondering where a man could find a Dreki around here?"

Rolf was stunned. The Dreki was a secret, wasn't it? Known to only a few? That's what he had assumed. Maybe not?

After a moment, in which he looked at the stranger with open mouth, he pointed straight down.

"Thank you kindly," said Egil, and climbed away.

Rolf sat scatterbrained and sleepy for a moment, watching the horn-headed man descend. And then he became overwhelmed with curiosity. After all, he had wished to make an impression on this man and all he'd managed to do was say two words, sounding like an idiot. Maybe he'd get another chance. After all, if he was smart and eloquent only in his own mind, or in the company of an empathetic leaf, was it really worth anything?

He decided there was nothing else to do but to follow the poet who had become for him a strange sort of mentor, keeping a discreet distance and sticking to the other side of the tree.

"Goodbye for now," he whispered to Idun and started to climb away. And then he came back and added, "I'll be back. Don't worry about that squirrel. I told him to stay away from this part of the tree."

And then he climbed away again.

"Goodbye!" called Idun as he went. "Farewell!" And because time goes by even quicker for a leaf than it does for a squirrel, she added, "Have a good life!" Rolf had already tried many times to explain that he would return, but it didn't matter even when he did, so he'd given up. Every parting for her was imbued with the sadness of forever. Every return a homecoming from the vasty world.

As Egil descended, it became darker and darker, and the trunk became damper and damper until he realized he was climbing over moss that caked the tree and was becoming slippery to the touch. At a certain point, he descended through a kind of earthen crust, like a potter's shallow bowl that stretched as far as the eye could see. And then he was beneath it and saw that it was a vast thing, cradled in the powerful limbs of the tree.

Still lower, he felt like he was no longer climbing on a living thing at all, but rather some kind of greasy stalactite, hanging down, joining up with its sister stalagmite below. Water dripped all around him, and the only living things he noticed down here were spiders and worms and the occasional mosquito.

And then his foot touched spongy ground and he sank into it up to the waist. He had come to the bottom.

All around him it was dark. He waded several yards through the goop, wondering whether he'd arrived in the realms of the dead. For a moment, he entertained the notion that his wife dwelled in some dark cave here, below the earth, as the Vikings and the Christians both believed.

"Nope," he said out loud. "I surely won't believe any kind of bogeyman claptrap like that. Me, I don't believe in Christian gods or Norse gods or any gods at all that would cart their sinners off to some stinking cold cave in the earth. Nor some hot cave neither. Not me. That's just stupid."

In the dusky black, he could make out an enormous rocky form close by, stretching a long way off into the distance. He put his hand against it. It felt knobby, like rock, but rough too, like bark.

And then he saw a sinkhole in the mossy earth, wisps of smoke rising from it, and he said to himself, "Where else would I hide if I were a large lizardy creature with a big hot brain that needs constant cooling and a furnace for a set of lungs? Where else but in the cool mossy damp of the deepest earth?"

And so he cleared his throat and prepared to speak like the poet he was.

But the Dreki spoke first.

"You are not supposed to be standing here before me," it said.

13

The Spy

ROLF WAS AFRAID of the dark, and was especially afraid to climb through the cracked shell of the crusty earth. He was afraid he might crack it further as he slipped through, like the clumsy oaf he was. He worried it would break like an egg and then the earth—if that's what it really was—would fall apart above his head. He was afraid, but still he managed to slide through without touching the edges, and then he arrived at the bottom.

And then, when he stepped into the moss, his leg sank all the way up to his thigh, and he thought, no, the worst thing would be for me to disappear forever and never see Freya again. No. Not his sister, he thought, banishing her face from his mind. Idun. Idun, the fragile leaf. It was her he would never see again.

And then his foot touched solid ground below the moss. And then he heard voices coming from somewhere in front of him, in the murky blackness. One of them he recognized. The other was as deep and low as anything he could possibly imagine. He wondered for a moment whether he was indeed imagining it. It had an impossible resonance, cadences that came from dreams. It was like a voice inside his head, wise and very tired.

They were in the middle or perhaps even near the end of a conversation. Rolf could not say what the conversation might have comprised, but it had clearly upset the man—Egil the Poet—who seemed to be huffing as if he'd been winded.

"Why do I get the feeling that you're lying to me?" Egil was saying.

"I do not lie," said the deep dark voice. *"Drekis do not lie. They might leave out certain facts, but they do not lie."*

"Those are called lies of omission," said Egil. "They are just like lies."

"No, they're not."

"Yes, they are."

"No."

"Yes."

"No."

"Yes."

It went back and forth like this for awhile. Rolf started to move closer and then changed his mind.

"I am going to use as many giants as I can to protect this tree."

"How is the tree in danger?"

"That is not for you to know."

"Maybe it's not in danger at all."

"It is in danger."

"Tell me how, or I will thwart all your efforts to protect it."

"You should not threaten me."

"I have nothing to lose by threatening you."

"Have you not seen the dead tree that lies beside this?"

"I have."

"Then allow it to be protected."

"You're a Dreki. Why can't you protect it yourself?"

"I cannot protect it myself."

"Why not?"

"Do you think I am going to reveal to you the ways in which I am weak?"

"So you are weak somehow," said Egil, and his voice was dripping with a bitterness that Rolf could not understand.

The poet went on. "I will find out. Maybe not now, but one day I will. You live here among darkness and smoke. Maybe it's to hide the fact that you are frail and small."

"Maybe," said the Dreki.

"Perhaps," said Egil, "you are weak and small because you came too early out of your cursed Dreki egg."

Rolf caught his breath, wondering how a poet could mock a Dreki.

"Don't tempt me," said the Dreki.

"That is exactly what I will do, Dreki. I will tempt you."

"Oh, will you?"

"I will."

"How?"

"I will climb back up to the middle of this tree and out through the waterfall and I will wait for these giants you say you have summoned."

"Really?"

"Yes, really. And when they come, those brutal and doltish creatures, I will ambush and kill them all. Don't think I can't do it either. I can. For I am a man with nothing to lose and that makes me a dangerous man and a berserker to boot . . ."

Rolf could barely hold his breath, but he had to, knowing if he let it loose it would come out in a gasp. His world had just turned upside down. Here he had begun to think this man could teach him something. He was a poet and Rolf wanted to learn about words. But Egil the Poet had just revealed himself to be an evil man, and he continued to speak in his half-crazed tone out there in the gloom, mocking and taunting the Dreki. Rolf had heard enough, though. This man was his enemy. Nothing had ever been so clear.

Gulping for air, Rolf grasped the slippery trunk and tried to pull himself quietly from the muck, which made terrible sucking sounds every time he moved. His hands flailed wildly about, looking for some purchase, and eventually he clutched at a vine that hung down and seemed willing to take his weight. Using all his strength, he pulled himself slowly out of the mossy goo and slid his feet along the snaky roots until a crevice gave him a foothold and allowed him to pull himself free. He thought he was making so much noise that he was moments away from being confronted by the berserker who would call him brutal and doltish and then kill him and probably laugh the whole time he was doing it too.

But Rolf was out of the muck and could hear no sign of pursuit. He felt around with his hand until he found a knot and, as deft as a child of average size, scrabbled swiftly up the tree and was gone. He was terrified of this poet who was going to foil all the plans of Idun and Rat-A-Task and the giants and himself. Somehow he knew he would have to prevent it.

14

The Twitch-Up Snare

AS ROLF CLIMBED as fast as he could up the tree, he tried to recall the feeling he'd felt while tossing Viking warriors hither and yon around the Field of Snorre. How long ago was that now? He didn't even know. In the Tree of the World, it is a fact, you lose all track of time. He tried to feel the feeling, but it didn't work and he knew why too. This man Egil was no bigger than any of those Vikings, but he was an enemy whom Rolf had once thought might be a friend. And that was the scariest thing of all.

He went up and up and up. He passed the crust of the earth and ascended through the needles and up into the leaves until the trunk itself began to narrow and seemed to sway under his weight.

He was out of breath from climbing. But he still had

to climb higher. The squirrel had been spending more and more time in these upper reaches of the tree. He said he could find the best twigs up here, for finishing touches on the drey. Rolf couldn't climb as high as Rat-A-Task could go, though he was now higher than he'd ever been and saw things he'd never seen before. Glassy cocoons and tricoloured ants and wispy clouds that drifted by in the blue above. He did not have time to linger over them, though; he had to find the little squirrel.

When he'd got as far as he could, he even thought he caught a glimpse of a pair of bronze wings spreading in the oblique rays of the setting sun high above him. He saw a flash of feather and then he thought he saw the cruel visage of an enormous hawk perched way up there.

The sight of the hawk reminded Rolf of Morton, and his heart burst for a moment at the thought that perhaps Freya's old falcon was really alive again, and that he'd had his wings restored, and that he was soaring up there in the blue.

But then this hawk twisted its haughty head over to one side and Rolf caught its eye—cold, imperious, curious in a predatory way. Probably wondering whether Rolf, who must have looked tiny among the branches of the Tree of the World, might make a tasty evening meal. Not like Morton at all then. Still, it nearly made him forget his task.

And then a red flash of bushy tail brought him to himself. "What are you doing way up here?" asked Rat-A-Task. "Wait," he added, pointing to a collection of twigs and leaves. "Before you answer, take those and fill those big pockets of yours."

"We're in trouble," said Rolf, filling his pockets.

"Nonsense," said the squirrel. "Everything is going swimmingly."

"Not if you can't swim," said Rolf impatiently.

"I don't mean truly," retorted the squirrel. "It's a metaphorical statement, favoured by scholarly squirrels such as myself. And you are covered in mud."

Rolf looked down himself and realized that indeed he was filthy from sinking into the swill at the root of the tree. For a moment he was embarrassed and ashamed for not being a well-kempt boy. He wondered if this was the reason giants had a reputation for being ugly and stupid. Perhaps they were busy running around with urgent messages and took no notice of their appearance.

But then he recalled the urgency of his own message.

"I don't care if I'm covered in mud!" he said. "And I don't care either about the grammar your mother taught you!" He was shouting as bossily as his sister ever had. "There is real trouble coming from below!"

A tail swished and in a blink Rat-A-Task was on Rolf's shoulder. "Tell me," he said.

"There's a man down there who's going to kill the giants!"

"What man?"

"The man we saw in the woods! Egil the Poet! He wants to kill the giants and hurt the tree!"

"He wants to hurt the tree?" said the squirrel. And Rolf could see how his expression suddenly became serious, cruel, and hard. "Why?"

"I don't know for sure," said Rolf, "but I suspect he just likes to fill the lives of others with misery! For his own entertainment!"

"That's a hard one," said Rat. "You can't change a mind that likes to be contrary with any kind of scholarly argument."

"No," said Rolf. "I don't think so. He wasn't even afraid of the Dreki."

"You saw the Dreki?" asked the squirrel. He sounded suddenly suspicious.

"I heard him," said Rolf.

"Did you speak to him?"

"No!" said the giant. "He didn't know I was there! Don't worry! I'm not going to try and take your place as the most important squirrel of the Tree of the World. I'm not even a squirrel!"

"That's true," said the squirrel, reassuring himself as he combed his own tail with his paw. "You're not even a squirrel."

"Could we please just get back to the matter at hand?" asked Rolf. "We have to stop this man. We have to trap him. But he's stronger and smarter and older than us."

"It can be done," said the squirrel. "We will trap him with the help of the tree."

"How?" asked Rolf. "A net? That's how we captured

Morton the hawk."

"Not a net," said Rat-A-Task, using his tail now to brush the fur on his ears. "That's for birds. We need to make ourselves a good old-fashioned snare."

"A snare?"

"Yes," said the squirrel, and his eyes twinkled mischievously. "It's what they use to catch squirrels!"

"Oh!" said Rolf, shocked enough to recoil a bit and start the high branch swaying beneath his weight. "Have you seen one?"

"No. But my mama described them to us in great detail, so we'd know to avoid them."

"Oh," said Rolf. "But this would have to be much bigger than a snare designed to catch a squirrel."

"Oh, yes," said Rat. "Yes, indeed. In which case, it helps a bit to be sitting inside the biggest tree in the world. Now," he added with sly pleasure, "we have to start right away if we're going to catch a giant-killer! First we need to find a log. It has to be an old log. A new piece of wood might have sap seeping out of it that will stick it to its place in the knothole."

"What knothole?" asked Rolf.

"You'll see!" shouted the squirrel, in his little voice. "So we need a log. An old log. Listen to me now and I will tell you: Out on the plateau behind the waterfall, that's where you'll find some. I saw them on our way in. They must have been sitting there for generations, must have been stacked by someone who lived, once, right there, on the plateau! Can you imagine? He was a man, but he was living like a squirrel in a high place that he had to climb to at the end of every day! He must have felt so safe. And he collected wood and built fires there at night that must have been seen for hundreds of miles. And then one day he departed and left behind him many logs. They're almost petrified. Perfect for our purposes."

The squirrel was scurrying from branch to branch, down through the tree, past the plateau and down and down. Rolf followed him.

"What are you looking for now?" he asked, trying with some difficulty to keep up with the deft and tiny squirrel.

"A knothole!" cried the squirrel. "All our fortune lies in the finding of a well-placed knothole! But I'm sure I've seen one. Ah! Right here!"

And then he performed the joyful little squirrel dance that Rolf had seen before.

The squirrel now began to exhort Rolf to examine the knothole and remember its dimensions so that he'd be able to select a log that would wedge into it exactly. Too small and it would not work. Too big and it would be no use at all.

"But how does it work?" asked Rolf. "The trap?" He was nervously looking around. They were close to Idun's little leaf area, her little collection of fragile branches. Rolf always began to get nervous when the squirrel got close to Idun. Leaves in general were mostly so much insulation to him, even if he never plucked a living one.

"All we have to do," said the squirrel, a glint in his little eye, "is find a bough, somewhere above us here, thick enough to be strong and thin enough to bend easily. We'll pull it into a curve, and when it's good and taut, we'll tie one end of our rope to it and make the other end into a slip knot loop with a dangling end that we'll tie to the log you've found. Then we'll shove the log into the knot, wedge it in well enough that it will hold the curved branch—just barely. But also so that it will look like a good foothold to a climber. Then the climber will come along, and as he climbs past the knot, he'll step on the foothold, his foot will catch the loop, the log will fall out of its hole, the bough will snap back to its place, and there you'll have your giant-killer, hanging upside down and dangling, caught by one foot."

"And then what?"

"What do you mean, and then what? And then he won't be able to harm a squirrel, much less a giant."

"But then he'll be in a predicament himself. How will we get him out of that?"

"Why do you want to get him out?"

"I mean, after we convince him not to hurt anybody."

"Look, friend," said the squirrel. "You came to me to help you catch a giant-killer. I'm not interested in dispensing advice on how to set him free. You should talk to some other squirrel if you want to do that."

"I don't know any other squirrel," said Rolf.

"Very well, then. You have your answer. We shall

leave him where he is. And look: just the bough—the proper length, thickness, and pliability."

Rolf followed the little squirrel's eye line, straight up, past the knothole in the tree and toward a nice curving branch that ascended beautifully from a round little hovel against the trunk. Rolf knew the hovel well because it's where Idun was.

Idun! Idun was growing out of a tiny twig that itself grew out of the very bough that Rat-A-Task proposed to curve and tie and snap.

"What if we harm the tree?" asked Rolf.

"We cannot harm this tree," said the squirrel, laughing. "No one can harm the tree *that* easily."

Rolf felt a fit of temper coming on. "SO WHY HAVE I BEEN CALLED UPON TO PROTECT A TREE THAT CANNOT BE HARMED," he shouted, and realized that Rat-A-Task had scurried a hundred feet above him along the trunk. "Sorry," he called, more gently. Still, he was angry. He wanted his concerns to be taken seriously.

"You can't harm it, Rolf. You. You cannot harm it alone. There are those who could, but not you or me or this single man. The Tree of the World is too big."

"Some parts of it are very small," said Rolf.

"Which parts?" asked the squirrel.

"Certain branches, certain twigs, certain . . . leaves."

Rolf felt his love was as glaring and obvious as his blushing. But the squirrel didn't notice a thing.

"What do leaves matter?" Rat-A-Task said, laughing

again. He had travelled almost all the way back to where Rolf was waiting for his answers.

"Certain leaves matter," said Rolf. "And so all leaves matter."

"Pshaw," said the squirrel.

"It's just—" said Rolf, and Rat-A-Task laughed now at his blushing, though he didn't know what was causing it. "THERE'S A PARTICULAR LEAF!" Rolf shouted finally. "I LIKE THE LOOK OF IT SO YOU WILL NOT TOUCH IT!"

He had not exactly spoken the truth, but it had the desired effect.

"Oh," Rat-A-Task called from thirty yards up the tree, his eyes wide and luminous. And then he shrugged. "Well, why didn't you say so?" And he scurried back down. "Where is this leaf?"

Rolf was embarrassed, but finally he pointed to where Idun grew.

"Oh there," said the squirrel. "That leaf is perfectly safe. Look how close it is to the base of the tree. Even if the bough breaks from the weight of the rope or the man, the broken part will be so far along the branch that your leaf will not even feel a tremor."

"Are you sure?" asked Rolf. Waves of relief were spilling over him.

"Absolutely sure," said the squirrel. And he barely restrained himself from rolling his eyes as he added, "Your precious little leaf will not be harmed."

Rolf was so relieved that he endured the embarrassment of Rat's mockery. And he also laid aside the question of what they might do with Egil once the poet had been captured.

All that had to be done now was the log had to be collected and the snare had to be built. There were other questions, like how would they form the slip knot so that it was open wide enough for a foot to slide into it, rather than hanging limp and closed like two pieces of rope side by side. What was the answer to that, you may ask.

"Easy," said Rat-A-Task, his eyes glinting in the now growing dark. "You collect old spiderwebs and use little bits of them to make the sides of the loop cling to the edges of the knot, wide open."

Wide open. They were going to make what the squirrel called a twitch-up snare.

"Should we wait till morning?"

"No, we should do it now."

So then Rolf climbed up and out onto the slippery plateau in the growing dark. He walked to the lip, crouched, and peered over the edge, feeling the spray of the water against his cheeks. Out here, in the wide open space of the world, Rolf felt strangely smaller than he did in the embrace of the tree. The tree was a protective place, the world outside was not.

He allowed his eyes to adjust to the spaces between the falling water and looked down, down, to the bank of the river below, where he saw a scrum of trees full of crows, cawing and laughing. On the other side, there was a jagged rock, jutting over the bright water. There he saw the dark figure of a man, sitting with his legs crossed and concentrating on something in his lap.

It was The Beaky. Rolf was sure of it. The friendly Beaky, sitting by the river and sewing something. Rolf considered for a moment shouting down to him. But then he felt the old shyness again, afraid if he called down, he would not be able to utter more than a single word, a single syllable even. That would be no fun at all. So he did not call down. Still, he was curious. What was The Beaky doing there? Two horses were there as well, tied among the trees beyond the clearing.

The sky was darkening fast, so Rolf shook off his questions, collected a trio of good-sized logs, in case one wasn't the right size, and made his way back down into the tree, where the squirrel was waiting for him with a fine collection of spiders' threads.

It was quick work to build the trap, though when they were finished, it was pitch dark. Then they climbed back up into the half-built drey and slept until dawn, secure in the knowledge that their plan would work.

Rolf slept and had a dream that he'd dreamt many times before, about climbing up into the Tree of the World, toward the sun, and seeing all the insects and animals and leaves and fungi. And then he saw Morton, the hawk. He was standing in a clearing in the woods with Freya. Rolf was there too, but they weren't looking at him. The hawk was akking at the sister, as he often did, only now Rolf found that he could understand what he was saying. "Round and round I go," he was saying, and his voice was plaintive, sad. "Snared by fate. Tied to the Tree of the World and whirling around it, caught in some wild, infernal wind that will never stop until the tree topples and all things come to an end!"

And then Rolf woke, eyes wide, realizing it wasn't a dream so much as a memory from the day when he and his sister had first met the wise and grizzled hawk, when Morton had told them he was in flight from the king, when everything in their lives had changed forever. How long ago had that been? Was it still only a few days?

He felt the squirrel's small body breathing deeply against his neck, as they lay there in the huge scooped bottom of the drey. It was just before dawn.

15

Mind Games

DOWN IN THE DEPTHS, where none of Rolf's spying or fleeing had been perceived, the conversation between Egil the Poet and the Dreki had begun somewhat differently from what the giant boy had heard. It's true, our Egil was a bit crazy, but there are things you already know about Egil that Rolf does not: specifically, that Egil the Poet was suffering from a broken heart. Even if broken hearts cannot be mended, the destructive ways that go along with them can. Or perhaps they can.

When Egil had first climbed down into the depths beneath the earth's crust where the old dead tree had sunk, the Dreki had known him immediately, and so had spoken up.

"You are not supposed to be standing here before me," the Dreki had said.

"What do you mean?" Egil had answered.

"You are Egil the Poet, yes?"

Egil was surprised. But he answered. "Yes."

"You were supposed to encounter the sons of Erik Blood-Axe. Did this encounter not take place?"

It took Egil a moment to recall how a Dreki is said to know the past and the future in the same way you and I might move back and forth in the story of a book simply by turning its pages. So it was true then. But why would this Dreki care about such an event as his encounter with the Haralds?

"The encounter did indeed take place," he replied.

"You fought with them?"

"I did."

"Seven against one?"

"I believe that was the number."

"They were meant to defeat you. If you are here, in front of me, then I do not understand. Which is itself a paradox since I am supposed to understand everything."

I have to try, for the first time ever, to explain the mind of a Dreki, despite the fact that I barely understand it myself. This creature was being presented with evidence that his memory for past and future had somehow become flawed. He didn't panic, though. Experience from a long (and perhaps multiple) lifetime had taught him that such a glitch often was something very small, if it could be overlooked so easily, and had a simple explanation—like when you skip a step in a math problem and get the wrong answer. Or, if you prefer a less terrifying example, like the way a mirror leaning up against a wall can seem to be an open door.

The Dreki could only conclude that there was such a kink in his vision of Egil's recent past. Something which, when he found it, could be ironed out in such a manner that everything would smooth back into place, making the Dreki once again master of the future.

"Did you thwart them in their task?" asked the Dreki, referring again to Egil's encounter with the Haralds.

"If you mean did I stop them from going out and collecting a battalion of giants, no, I did not."

"Well," said the Dreki, almost sounding relieved. *"That is a good thing."*

"Why?" asked Egil. "What if I did? What is that to a Dreki?"

"I am the primary instigator of their quest."

"That's funny. I thought it was a giant who instigated their quest—yet another kind of being I did not believe existed before today."

"That giant was manipulated by a squirrel who was in turn manipulated by me. I am the protector of this tree."

"I see," said Egil, although he wondered why the Dreki would use the word "manipulated." He felt as if this Dreki was lying to him. It seemed to him that anyone who was aware he was "manipulating" his fellow creatures, instead of just convincing them of the rightness of a task, was probably up to no good. Perhaps this Dreki was not choosing his words carefully because he was upset about this puzzle he had been confronted with. Perhaps he was so busy thinking about it that he was forgetting to "manipulate" Egil.

"So you did not kill the sons of Erik Blood-Axe?"

"Of course not," said Egil. "They were just children."

"Children?" asked the Dreki. *"This is a strange kind of boast. Is it not common for men such as you to exaggerate your exploits, along with the fearsomeness of your enemies, rather than play them down?"*

Egil shrugged. "They were children," he said. "Nothing to boast about."

"Ah ha," said the Dreki. *"Is it not itself a boast to say there is nothing to boast about?"*

"You got me there," said Egil, who didn't know what the Dreki was going on about. "Though if you ask me, I'd say you're a bit confused."

It was true. The Dreki was confused. Possibly the only state of mind he was unfamiliar with. Perhaps the Dreki should have considered how this word *children* might have been a clue to the kink in his vision—the evidence that he was looking at a mirror leaning against a wall instead of through a doorway. But he was too concerned about the deep mystery of Egil's character, suddenly unknowable to him, to understand what it meant for a Dreki not to know that the sons and daughters of Erik Blood-Axe were really children. He believed the sons and daughters of Erik Blood-Axe were big strapping adults who had been pillaging across Denmark and making war. It did not occur to him that the sons and daughters of Erik Blood-Axe had only been making *believe* they were making war, because they were children; that Erik Blood-Axe had not brought them to battle on the Field of Snorre, because they were children; that Erik had kept them in a safe place, a snow-covered yard on the grounds of his longhouse, surrounded by a high fence, where they had split up into two groups and pretended to make war with one another. Because they were children. That Erik had allowed them to stay behind in Norway despite the fact that they were children, because he was an old defeated man who did not want to destroy their Viking spirit.

It did not occur to the Dreki that Egil had defeated the sons and daughters of Erik Blood-Axe so easily because he was a grown man and they were children. He simply thought Egil was boasting.

How could a Dreki be so wrong about this? I'm afraid I cannot tell you now. It is a subject for another book. I'm sorry about that, I'm going as fast as I can, doing my best, despite the fact I have aching in my finger-joints, writing does not come naturally to me, and technically speaking I'm more than a thousand years old.

Ahem. Back to Egil and the Dreki.

The Dreki was speaking to a man who was supposed

to be dead, killed by the overwhelming force of the sons of Erik Blood-Axe. Since he was dead, there wasn't supposed to be anything left to know about him.

So then *what* was Egil the Poet doing here, at the black root of the Tree of the World?

The problem for a Dreki who thinks that everything is foreordained is he can never know how a person *might* behave. He's too busy knowing how they *will* behave. *Might* is impossible, for a Dreki. It adds to his confusion. Makes him feel finite, mortal, vulnerable. Panicky.

"Go back to Iceland," he said simply.

"I will not," said Egil. "There is nothing for me there."

"Your family," said the Dreki, remembering something he knew. *"They are all dead."*

"A volcano," said Egil, between gritted teeth.

"Regrettable. Except it was not quite a volcano."

"I beg your pardon?"

"Your family was not killed by a volcano."

"Yes, I heard you. But what did you mean? If my family wasn't killed by a volcano, then what, oh hidden one, cowering beneath your wisps of smoke in this bog, were they killed by?"

The Dreki paused and then spoke.

"As I said before, you should not be here in this tree. You should have been killed by the sons and daughters of Erik. So I will do the next best thing and drive you away. I shall do this by dispiriting you. So I will tell you. Your family was not killed by a volcano. Though it looked like a volcano, sounded like a

146

volcano, and felt like a volcano, it was not a volcano."

"Get to the point!" shouted Egil, more despairing than impatient.

"Regrettably," said the Dreki, *"your family was killed by the birth of a Dreki."*

Egil could not believe his ears. "What do you mean?"

There was silence from the smoke-seeping hole.

"What do you mean!" Egil shouted again, and his words reverberated up through the trunk of the tree, almost finding the giant ears of Rolf, who unfortunately had not yet arrived quite within earshot. Though the boy did feel a tremor all the same.

"Or, more a rebirth than a birth."

"Enlighten me," said Egil coldly.

"Gladly. You see, a Dreki lays an egg full of liquid ore. If it cracks too early, before the ore is absorbed by the Dreki growing within, then the ore will come seeping out."

"A premature Dreki birth?"

"Indeed."

"But—" sobbed Egil, feeling his heart break all over again. "It covered hundreds of acres!"

"I am sorry. The birth of a Dreki is not supposed to kill anyone. But the premature birth of a Dreki is something that cannot be foreseen. And when this particular egg was first buried several of your generations ago, that island was an abandoned place. Of course, the mother Dreki knew the island would become populated, but . . ."

"Iceland?"

147

"Yes."

"Was it you?"

"I was the premature Dreki, yes."

"You killed my family?"

"I offer as consolation the fact that, one day in the future, the earth will be so populated, it will be impossible to lay a Dreki egg anywhere at all. And so we will become extinct."

"Good," said Egil. "I'm glad."

"Perhaps now, however, you are dispirited and will go away?"

Egil realized all of a sudden, even though the Dreki had told him as much, that this creature was attempting to manipulate him. The thought dried up his tears and made his blood run cold in his veins.

"Why do I get the feeling that you're lying to me?" he asked finally (and this part—in case it has slipped your mind—was overheard by Rolf).

"I do not lie," said the Dreki. *"Drekis do not lie. They might leave out certain facts, but they do not lie."*

"Those are called lies of omission," said Egil. "They are just like lies."

"No, they're not."

"Yes, they are."

"No."

"Yes."

"No."

"Yes."

"You are simply not supposed to be here at all. I cannot manipulate you. I cannot even say what it is you are going to do."

"But what are *you* going to do?"

"I am going to use as many giants as I can to protect this tree."

"How is the tree in danger?"

"That is not for you to know."

"Maybe it's not in danger at all."

"It is in danger."

"Tell me how, or I will thwart all your efforts to protect it."

"You should not threaten me."

"I have nothing to lose by threatening you."

"Have you not seen the dead tree that lies beside this?"

"I have."

"Then allow it to be protected."

"You're a Dreki. Why can't you protect it yourself?"

"I cannot protect it myself."

"Why not?"

"Do you think I am going to reveal to you the ways in which I am weak?"

"So you are weak somehow," said Egil. "I will find out. Maybe not now, but one day I will. You live here among darkness and smoke. Maybe it's to hide the fact that you are frail and small."

"Maybe," said the Dreki.

"Perhaps," said Egil, "you are weak and small because you came too early out of your cursed Dreki egg."

"Don't tempt me."

Egil was feeling bitter now. And destructive. Self-destructive. If this Dreki was going to be manipulative, perhaps he could be manipulative too.

"That is exactly what I will do, Dreki. I will tempt you."

"Oh, will you?"

"I will."

"How?"

"I will climb back up to the middle of this tree and out through the waterfall and I will wait for these giants you say you have summoned."

"Really?"

"Yes, really. And when they come, those brutal and doltish creatures, I will ambush and kill them all. Don't think I can't do it either. I can. For I am a man with nothing to lose and that makes me a dangerous man and a berserker to boot . . ."

Here, you may recall, is where the young, impressionable Rolf ran away. Or rather climbed away, fleeing in horror from this vision of Egil the giant-slayer. What Egil said next changed the meaning of what he'd just spoken, however. And so it's too bad Rolf did not hear it.

". . . so if you don't want any of that to happen," Egil continued, "you might want to obliterate me right now with a big belch of that Dreki breath, just like you did to my family."

"You would not kill innocents," said the Dreki.

"You said yourself you don't know anything about me."

The Dreki laughed then. A long, painful low screech of a laugh, full of mockery.

"You are Egil, the poet," he said, *"enemy of Erik Blood-Axe. Former speaker of terrible verses, who learned, through tragedy, to speak better. Though you do not care anymore about how a person speaks. You care only about how a person behaves. You would not kill innocents, will not kill innocents even if they are giants. Your future may be unmoored from my memory, but I know your past. And past, as the politicians say, is prologue. Your past is full of virtue—reckless virtue, perhaps, but virtue nonetheless—virtue conducted in memory of a wise and faithful wife, whom you love even though she is dead and gone, buried under the lava that covered the Icelandic earth."*

Egil did not want to hear one more word about his virtue or his future or his past or his beloved wife. Full of bitterness and rage, he fled from that dark hole where the faceless Dreki hid, scampering back over the thick roots snarled in muck and brine, till his hands grasped onto bark and he began to climb back up the glorious Tree of the World, weeping like a child.

16

Everything Upside Down

EGIL FLEW UP through the tree like a startled woodpecker. He climbed so fast that he did not watch where he was going and knocked his head on the first large limb to loom up in his path, driving the horn of his helmet so far into the wood that it was not going to be easy to pull out. He clung there, head ringing from the blow, cursing the clumsiness of the tree, the horn, anything but himself. Eventually he realized he was going to need some serious leverage to get the horn out, and so he placed his feet on either side of his object, sideways against the trunk, gripped the helmet in both arms, and pulled as hard as he could. After five attempts, the horn finally popped out like a cork from a bottle, sending Egil flying down into the depths of the tree from whence he'd come. He fell so fast he could barely even snatch at the branches. They lashed him all the way until he finally plummeted through the hole in the crust and landed headfirst in the stinky mulch beneath.

Now Egil had a new problem, since he had plunged well past his shoulders into the goo, with his feet sticking straight up, and he could not breath. But the swamp was snagged all over with old dead roots and Egil was able to grip one, first with his foot, and then bend at the waist and curl his whole body up and around it, whereupon he pulled himself out, gasping and coughing. The smell and the rot of the mulch had gotten so far up his nose that he fainted for a spell. When he woke, he was disoriented for a few moments, unsure of where he was. He was still holding the single-horned helmet in his two hands. As he put it on his head, his memory returned. He realized he was back in the proximity of the Dreki, and that there was nothing he wanted more than to get away.

So Egil set off again, sprang into action just as carelessly as before, and began to climb. Up through the crust he went, and over the needly branches, past the offending limb whose wound was already dripping with the sap that would heal it, and up and up into the tree, where night had fallen.

He'd been climbing for awhile, not the least bit calmed despite his setbacks. He didn't have any idea where he was in his climb. If he had given it any thought, it might have occurred to him that the wisest course of action in the deepening darkness would be to find a wide bough and bed down against the trunk until morning.

But Egil wanted to get out from among all these branches and foliage, beloved of this destructive Dreki and his minions, numberless, nameless, and watchful, who dwelled within the tree and fed off its gifts. He wanted to go home, even though he had no home. He wanted to disappear into the dark wintry woods of Norway. Find somewhere to lie down and die. This Dreki had killed his family, just by being born. Or reborn, as the case may be. And Egil hated him, not so much for being born but for telling him of it so callously, so chillingly. With such malice. For no reason at all. He would be revenged on the Dreki somehow.

Egil was an expert climber and did not have to think about what he was doing in order to do it. So when his foot found a hold in a knothole of the tree that was just like any other knothole his foot had ever found, he swung himself up into the next handhold and then he pulled away. Just like always. Only this time the results were different. A bough alongside him snapped away, somewhere in the darkness, flinging itself into the ether.

And, much to Egil's surprise, he snapped away too. He flew out with a powerful lash that swung him upside down and dangling from his ankle before he even had a chance to cry out or think another thought. Around him, several branches began to sway, as if objecting to the tree's complicity in his entrapment. But really it was just what you would call gravity. Weights and counterweights and swinging boughs. And then, as Egil swung out as far as he could go and then back, he was nearly impaled by a small broken branch that caught him in the side. The pain of it prevented him from grasping at the trunk to try and hold himself there, and then he swung out again, wheezing with pain and dripping blood.

And back again. This time he tried to take hold of the small sharp branch that had wounded him, but his hand could not find it in the dark. And so again he swung out, not so far this time, and then back, not so far again, and finally found himself dangling helplessly in the middle of the empty air, with nothing at all to hold him to the world except for the sharp tug at his left ankle, somewhere above him in the dark. And a wind whipping in his ears that might only have been the rush of his own blood from thrumming heart to aching head.

As he dangled there, Egil realized his sword had slipped out of his belt, fell swickering and swacking back down into the depths where the watchful, murderous Dreki dwelled. And his helmet had tumbled too.

"Hope you get your eyes poked out!" Egil shouted, even as he hung there. "One at a time! First by my sword and then by my horn! Perhaps that's why my good dog made off with that bone in happier times. So that I might one day put out the eye of a Dreki!"

And then he stilled himself. Hung quietly through the night and into the dawn. In the first light he felt the warmth creep over him, opened his eyes, and saw this new world that had taken his freedom.

"Look at that," he muttered, pretending things were normal. "A tree looks the same upside down as it does right side up. Nothing special there." And so he closed his eyes again and tried to shut the world out and himself down. He concentrated so hard on it that he did not notice the giant boy climb down from somewhere far above to take a hard look at him, open his mouth to speak, change his mind, turn pale, and, frightened, climb away.

And so Egil hung silently but would not shut down. The creeping dawn turned into morning. And morning kept creeping until it crept its way to the full light of day. And Egil still hung from the tree, arms folded and frowning, eyes closed and wide awake. Stubbornly he remained, like a pod hanging from a thread. A cocoon. But a cocoon is a hopeful thing—symbol of youth and future and life. Egil hung rather like a dead thing, waiting only for the darkness to fall forever.

"Hello?" said a voice. Egil assumed he was imagining it.

"Hello?" said the voice again. It was very small, but clear as a raindrop on your cheek. There was no doubt it was speaking to him.

"Hello," said Egil finally, wearily and painfully, since he was nothing if not polite.

"Hello!" the voice said again, delighted this time, though no less small. "So you're there. Are you there?"

"I am here," said Egil, as if to say "Where else in the world would I possibly be?" He creaked his throbbing head around. On one side of him there was the massive trunk; above and below him, all out of reach, there were many boughs and branches, leaves both wide and thin and needles too, below the top of his head—all of them shimmering in the light and low breeze that always seemed to swirl around the tree. Behind him, some ways away, was the dark shale of the inner cliff wall, obscuring the enormous tree from the sight of those who might be out walking the snowy Norwegian coast.

"Who are you?" asked the voice.

"I am Egil," said Egil. "Egil the Poet." He was becoming accustomed to this new half life wherein he was always having conversations with creatures he could not see.

"Hello, Egil. Where is Rolf?"

"Who is Rolf?" asked Egil.

"Rolf the Ranger, a boy who misses his family and so takes care of me," said the voice. "You don't know him? He is enormous, just like you. Maybe even more enormous. Though he does not hang upside down like you do. Do you like to hang upside down like that?"

"On certain days," said Egil. "Not today, though."

"Why not today?"

"It's giving me a splitting headache today. And it's

hurting my ankle. It's preventing me from eating or dying."

"Then why are you there?"

"I'm not doing this by choice," Egil said, annoyed. "I was only joking about that. Surely you can see that, if you've got eyes in your head. Somebody snared me. They caught my foot in a noose and left me to hang here."

"How awful," said the voice.

"Whatever," Egil replied, even though it might seem like the phrase of a later time.

"I shall help you to escape," said the voice.

"Really," said Egil. "Thank you, but that's not necessary. Don't worry about me. You should be on your way."

"On my way? But I'm not going anywhere," said the voice. "I am always here. I am a leaf. My name is Idun. How do you do."

"How do you do," said Egil surprised. And then, "I've never met a leaf." He spoke sadly and doubtfully, not without some irony. He felt he was going mad. First a giant. Then a Dreki. Now a leaf. What was the world coming to?

"I am farther up the branch you're tied to," said the leaf, "closer to the trunk. I can feel you—the vibration of you, and perhaps the weight of you too—hanging at the end of the branch. The bough communicates it to me. It does not feel right for you to be there. We are going to try and work you free."

"We?" asked Egil.

"The bough you're tied to, and the branches that grow from it, one of which is part of me. You'll be happy to know we have already formulated a plan."

"Ecstatic," replied Egil. This leaf was nothing if not optimistic. Were all leaves optimistic? Probably. "Anyway," he added, "I wish you all success in your efforts. I can't imagine my being here can be any more comfortable for you than it is for me."

"True, but that is only part of the reason," said the leaf. "I'm sure, if Rolf the Ranger were here, he would help you. He inspired me with the size of his heart. So I shall help you too."

"What can you do?" asked Egil, starting to tire of this conversation with a chipper twig. "I mean no disrespect, but if you're a leaf, I don't think you'll be much use to me, even if you have the help of a bunch of branches."

"And a bough," said the leaf.

"And a bough," said Egil. "Quite right." And nearly laughed despite his terrible state.

"As a leaf," said the leaf, "I feed the branch. I give it strength, strength which then passes into the bough it grows from. With my food—the food I make within myself from the light of the sun—I make them grow. Can you imagine? I make my food nearly out of thin air! What greater gift is there than to have such a skill! I'm the fuse and the force that makes the branch grow! And even the bough! And so we are going to grow our little branches out toward the knot that is tied to your foot. And we will grow through the knot and, with our little bit of pressure, we will make that knot come undone."

"Well, good luck," said Egil. "I expect to be dead by the time you succeed."

"Still, we will try. And we will go as fast as we can. Don't give up hope. I have to stop speaking to you now so that I can work."

"Very well," said Egil. "Good luck to you, getting rid of my dead weight, hanging here from your undeserving tree."

And so Egil hung there, in a new kind of silence, content to know that someone would one day cut him down, allow his body to fall, itself like an old leaf in the breeze, wafting into the depths. The shadows grew long and the quiet afternoon turned into evening. He heard birds twitter around him, and the sounds of rustling against the trunk and tried to make out what they must be. A family of moles, perhaps, for whom that part of the trunk was a hollow home, preferable to the damp cold of the snow-covered earth. Or perhaps it was a family of bats, rustling and chatting quietly, waiting patiently for night to fall so they could swing out and up and go about their blood-sucking business.

"Just don't go and tangle yourself in my hair," said Egil out loud. "You'll have a hard time getting out. It hasn't been combed in a while. My wife used to cut it and comb it too. Doesn't help that I've lost my helmet either. Doesn't help that I'm hanging upside down."

"I beg your pardon?" asked Idun the leaf.

"Oh, nothing," replied Egil. "Sorry to disturb."

"Not to worry!" called the leaf. "It is exhausting but satisfying labour." And indeed Egil did think he perceived a note of weariness creeping into her tone. If this was madness, he thought, it was a reasonable sort of madness. The company of a leaf. Was it so unlikely? Why couldn't there be a leaf here that spoke and dreamed and worked and was content with the fruits of its labour? The Tree of the World was an enormous thing, full of the wisdom of ages. Anything was possible within it, he supposed, beyond the bitter musings of a dying poet.

And so he hung, and so he thought, and so he imagined more conversations with the wildlife around him, the insects, and sometimes, he felt, the little atomies in the air. The first day stretched into the second and the second into the third, and it was clear to him that nothing would ever change.

"We have tried our best," said Idun, when she spoke to him again on the fourth day. "But we simply cannot poke it out."

Egil looked down or rather up at his feet. Sure enough, there was the wiry end of a branch there, snaking with the noose around his ankle.

"You did it!" he croaked. "I can't believe it. You grew all that way."

"But it has not helped," said Idun sadly. "We've been

trying now for the better part of a day, since we first arrived at your ankle. But that rope is tougher than the fibre of our being. And now I am weary. I am so weary. But I have another idea. I should have thought of it in the first place."

"What is it?" asked Egil, shocked by the sound of weariness, suddenly humbled by the little leaf's resourcefulness and courage. Even if that meant he had gone beyond mad. Even though he had become a man concerned about a leaf.

"Can you hang on much longer?" asked the leaf.

"Longer than my life, I'll wager," Egil replied. But he did not think she understood his bleak humour.

"This time we shall work faster," she sighed. "For it shall be the very branch I'm perched on that will grow. I shall guide it down toward your open hand. I have sensed the hands of Rolf the Ranger, he has cupped them around me, and he has done many other miraculous things as well. I should have thought of your hands and the work that you can do for yourself. It was selfish of me to think I could have accomplished it all. I sought to be the hero without any help from you. I am sorry."

"No!" croaked Egil, as tears welled inexplicably into his eyes and their drops fell into the darkness below. "You must not say that about yourself. You're a strong and brave little leaf. I underestimated you. I didn't even think you were really there, and maybe you're not, but it's clear anyway that you deserve my gratitude and respect. You, my friend, have the most heroic character of almost anyone I have ever met. I mean that honestly, little leaf."

"Nonetheless," said Idun, "there is much yet to be done. You must promise that when you feel the tip of my branch tickle the palm of your hand, you will close your fingers over it, and then pull yourself up, hand by hand, to the bough you're tied to. Do you promise to do that?"

"I promise," sighed Egil, closing his eyes and listening to the throbbing thunder of his five-days hung head.

"And then you shall be free. I cannot promise that we'll make it that far. If only I had thought of it before."

"Don't worry," said Egil. "You have come to the aid of an undeserving man, and if he survives he will compose an ode to the damsel Idun that the world will never forget."

But he mumbled the words, through parched lips, and the leaf did not understand them.

"Just hold on!" she cried. "We shall travel as fast as we can to arrive in your open hand. And then you must do the rest."

"Very well," said Egil. "Do your worst." And then he slept again.

He dreamt, as always, of the face of his wife, turning to him in the boat they'd used to travel to Iceland, her moon face surrounded everywhere by the blackness of the night, the black silver sway of the waves, and stars.

"You are going to be all right, Egil," said his wife.

And her voice was green and pretty and touched his ears like spring rain. "Hold out your hand," said his wife. And he did. He held out his hand to his wife and she placed her finger in it and poked him carefully in the palm. Poked it, right in the centre, with her nail.

Egil woke. He heard the voice of Idun, whose tone seemed now to be like that of a wise old woman.

"Now, sir, it is all up to you. We have spent our lives in this task. You cannot let us down now. Pull, Egil!"

Egil's half-hearted hand closed itself over the branch that, sure enough, had snaked its way into his palm. How many days had it been? He could not feel his feet, neither the bound one nor the one that dangled. Still, his left hand seemed to work and so too did his right. He swung around and felt a pain in his side. The wound. He pulled himself up, reached all the way around himself with his right hand—it was a long way—and grabbed the branch just below or rather above the handhold of his left. It was dewey and slim. He wondered whether it would snap from all his weight. No. It was sinewy. Tough. It would hold him.

He let go with his left, nearly losing his balance and spinning around on himself, twisting like a badly launched top, but managed to hold himself in place as he gripped again below or rather above his right hand's hold. As he did so, he felt a pain inside his chest that made him cry out with as much grief as anything else.

It was his heart, resisting this return to life.

"I don't care what you think!" said the mad poet now to his heart. "These creatures have devoted everything to set you free. You must oblige them."

And so, hand over hand under hand, hand by hand, slowly up the sinewy branch, Egil climbed. Bending up and over his unfamiliar looking legs, and then past them into the open and fresh scents of the tree. Until the back of his left hand grazed the underside of a much thicker bough, and he felt the bark that told him it was real.

He reached around and hugged it like he'd never held anything since his wife, first against his shoulder, and then closer to his chest. With his other hand he reached around the bottom of the bough and embraced it fully, with both arms, so it seemed like he was hugging himself. And then, afraid to loosen his body's passionate grip, he shimmied slowly, scratchily, painfully, around it until he lay panting on top of the bough and could release his full body's weight to it, like a child falling asleep on his mother's shoulder. Except this child was still closer to death than life, as his left foot dangled and throbbed below him, still waiting for the moment when it would finally be released, twisted and bloating, from its noose.

"Well done," said Idun, who seemed to be whispering now, right by his ear. Wearier too, she sounded, than Egil's own self. "Well done. And now you must remember to do one favour for me."

"Anything," breathed Egil.

"You must say farewell for me to my friend and protector, Rolf the Ranger, for I have reached the end of my life. I am going to die now."

"What?" asked Egil. And then, "Wait. What do you mean the end of your life?"

"It has been a long and full and satisfying life. And I have accomplished much. I have saved a creature that was a thousand times my size."

"Wait," croaked Egil, trying to pull himself up and see where the whisper was coming from. "Let me see you!"

"Farewell!" called Idun. "Remember, I will find earth! Or a home in a nest somewhere!"

And then, through bleary eyes, Egil saw a little yellow leaf drift by him, like a kite in the breeze. And then it fell. It had once tapered delicately to its point, but now it was curling around itself and dancing in the air.

"Farewell!" she called again. And her voice had no desire in it. Only satisfaction. "Remember!"

"I will," said Egil. "I will remember." And his clumsy hand reached out and tried to grasp the little yellow falling leaf that had come to mean so much to him. But it eluded his grasp and slipped away, drifting and falling into the darkness of the needling branches below.

"I hope you find earth," muttered Egil. "Or a nest somewhere." And then he began to cry. He cried for a long time as he clung to the bough. Wept like a baby. Mourned the loss of his own life. Until finally he fell asleep, still clinging to the bough, and slept a sweet dreamless sleep that did not wake him until he was ready to live again.

Though his rage was not so easily spent.

17

Despair

R OLF HAD HAD ENOUGH. He decided, against Rat-A-Task's protestations, that he had to set the hanging man free. He didn't know how much time had gone by, since the days in the tree always seemed to both fly by and go on forever.

"But he wants to kill giants!" yelled the little squirrel.

"So?" Rolf replied. "We'll tell him not to!"

"When? Before or after he's killed you?"

"Before he's killed me, of course," said Rolf. "Surely he would agree to that if I set him free."

"You can't change someone's mind so easily," said the squirrel. "Best to just let your enemies die off."

"Pah," said Rolf.

For Rolf, there was also the problem of not having been able to visit Idun, whom he missed terribly. He'd been afraid, since she was perched so close to the hanging man. The only way he'd be able to see her again was if he mustered the courage to go and set the man free.

But courage was something that Rolf still lacked.

Rat-A-Task was a red squirrel, which meant he was red all the time. At the moment though he was getting redder, if that was even possible. "I have an ambition!" he shouted. "You must not thwart my ambition!"

"I know," said Rolf, who knew better than to get between a creature and its ambition. "You want to be the Squirrel of the Tree."

"Exactly," said Rat. "And here we are, in the growing and greening Tree of the World, but I don't see any other squirrels here. Do you?"

"No," said Rolf, who didn't. "I want to help you," he continued. "You know I do. But what does my setting that hanging man free have to do with you delivering messages up and down the Tree of the World?"

Rat-A-Task scurried down the bough, along the branch just above Rolf's head, hopped down onto his shoulder, and looked him in the eye. "If this man kills all the giants, then there won't be anyone to protect the tree. The Dreki told me—the tree needs protectors, or else whoever chopped it down before will chop it down again! And that will leave me with precisely nothing at all! No task. No messages to take up and down the tree. Nothing."

"Who do you bring the messages from and to?" asked Rolf, suddenly curious about the details of the task.

"That," said the squirrel, somewhat imperiously, "is confidential information. Stop asking so many questions!"

Rolf could see that the squirrel's ambition gave him a bit of a mad glint in his eye. He never knew it was possible for a squirrel to look so much like his sister.

Still, he was confused. He told the squirrel not to worry. He promised he would not let the man kill any giants. And Rat-A-Task was satisfied, thinking this meant he was promising not to set the man free. The squirrel scurried back up into the interior of the drey, leaving Rolf to sit and think.

And sit and think he did. He didn't know what it was he should do, but it seemed cowardly and wrong to leave the man hanging there down in the middle regions of the tree. He thought it might help to make a decision if he saw with his own eyes what was happening. So he climbed down to take a look.

And that's when he found out that Egil was gone.

Egil the Poet and Giant-Killer was gone.

Suddenly the vast tree had become, to Rolf, a small and frightening place. Suddenly all the shadows and crevices and holes seemed inadequate and full of light. A place with more nooks and shadows and crevices and crannies than the whole of Norway felt suddenly like a wide open plain with nothing at all on it, and an earth-shaking herd of buffalo thundering toward him, as if he were standing many thousand miles west and a few hundred miles south of where he was.

Or worse. Every nook and cranny contained a giant-killer ready to spring.

Rolf sat very still on the branch above the branch above the bough in question and looked down at the empty space where the man had once been hanging. He would have to go down there and see if there was any clue that would tell him how long ago he had escaped. But what if the man was there, hiding just around the trunk of the tree? Waiting to ambush little Rolf and stab him in the heart?

Rolf was frightened. He sat for a long time. The leaves swayed in the breeze that always seemed to be blowing around the tree. He didn't know what to do.

Until he thought: Idun. I will ask Idun. His heart swelled with the thought that he could climb down and see the little leaf again, cup her in his palm, and soothe her until she stopped shivering. He knew that Idun would be able to tell him how long ago the man had escaped. Whether it was one forever or two forevers, or longer . . .

He was concerned too about the leaf. He had not seen her in so long. Slowly, slowly, he lowered himself down from the branch he was sitting on, to the next. And then down again to the next—putting the toe of his boot on it, then the whole of his foot. Then his second foot. Now he was in his favourite hollow and he turned and squatted, expecting to see Idun there.

But instead of Idun, there was another branch. A whole branch, growing narrowly out of the bough and hanging down. There was another thin branch too, a little further beyond this one, also long and hanging down, also unfamiliar and new.

Rolf thought maybe Idun was on the new branch somewhere, so he reached out as far as he could along the branch, lifted it up and examined each leaf all the way to the tip. The branch was pliant in his hands, supple, beyond a foot or two of stiffness near the joint where the branch met the bough. He examined the palmlike quality of each leaf—its colour and its axis and its midrib and its blade. There were plain leaves and leaves like shields and heart-shaped leaves that reminded him of the pounding of his own. They did not speak and anyway he already knew. There were compound leaves and elongated leaves and not one of them was Idun. Not one. He knew her sinuses and her contours and her teeth. The leaves he found were softly serrated, but they cut him nonetheless, because none of them were Idun.

Then he saw the twig she'd been attached to. Unmistakable. He saw the groove left by her stalk. It was hers all right, even though nothing was left of it but a scar. The scar of the leaf fallen from the stalk. It was dangling down near the place where the man would have been hanging.

Perhaps he had used it to climb up.

Perhaps he had wrenched away some of the leaves.

Rolf sat up like a bolt on the bough, so fast he nearly tumbled off it. But he caught himself, thinking hard. Egil the Poet, whom he had once feared but now only hated—Egil the Poet, killer of giants, had escaped his fate and killed Idun in the process. He had crushed her with his hand or torn her with his fingers and tossed her into the brackish belowparts, down where the knees of the tree were, and the octopus of its root system.

Egil the Poet had been selfish and careless and murderous. He had killed the creature whom Rolf had sworn to protect—the creature he cared for the most in a world where he had lost his sister and his father and, even, at the very beginning, his mother, and had become attached to a squirrel whose intentions he could never entirely understand or trust. A tender leaf had died. Somebody was going to be punished for her death.

Rolf did not know what he was doing. He climbed back up to the drey. Rat-A-Task was there. The squirrel came out and was about to leap onto Rolf's shoulder, but then he sensed that Rolf was different. Rolf was dangerous.

"The man escaped," said Rolf, with a sob.

"What?" shouted Rat-A-Task. "What? The man escaped? It's a disaster!"

"Disaster," answered Rolf, in his long-lost singular manner. No more thoughts, he felt, could be communicated with words. Only deeds. Giant deeds. Giant, murderous deeds. He did not wonder anymore whether anyone would approve or disapprove of his thoughts and behaviour. He did not wonder if Freya would think he had changed if she saw him, or if she thought he was smart. He was no longer pleased with his graduation from single words to stupid, eloquent sentences.

He just wanted to inflict disaster back on the man who had inflicted disaster on him.

Disaster. Here, thought Rolf, was a three-quarters built drey. But what use was there in building a drey when there was nothing for the drey to protect? The drey was never going to protect Idun. It was for indoor dwellers, like squirrels and poets and men. And for doltish, brutal giants like Rolf who did not keep the promises they'd made to fragile little leaves. In such a place, Idun was destined to be used only for insulation.

Rolf was careful not to mention the death of the leaf to Rat-A-Task because he knew the squirrel would not understand. Never in a million squirrel lifetimes would he understand. Even though the squirrel had promised that Idun would be safe and that nothing would ever happen to her in the twitch-up snare. Nothing.

But squirrels, like men and like all indoor dwellers with their houses of leaves or bricks or wood, were not to be trusted. Rolf was feeling feral, was beginning to see himself as an outdoor dweller, like a leaf or a tree. He was ready to grow fur. He wanted to tear the drey apart, so that the squirrel would feel as lonely and despairing and angry as he did. He wanted the squirrel to cling to his hair and bite his ear and try to stop him as he shredded the drey into the tree parts and twigs and human parts and the wool and the fur bits from which it came. He wanted to hurl it back into the chaos from whence it came. He wanted the squirrel to enter into the fury that he felt so that he would not be alone.

But he was alone.

"I'm going to see the Dreki," he said.

"What?" said Rat-A-Task. "No! You must not! He's dangerous. He doesn't like to be disturbed. He—"

"He gives you the reasons for things, yes? He knows the future, yes?"

"Yes," said the squirrel. "But—"

"I'm going to see him. And then I am going to come back. And there is no need for you to worry about that man, Egil the Poet. I am four times his size and he has something to fear from me."

"But—" said Rat-A-Task.

"I will give you the choice then, friend: Either I go see the Dreki or I tear apart your winter drey."

As he climbed down into the needly darkness, tears stinging his eyes, Rolf remembered all the lonely and bitter things that had ever happened in his life, before Idun's death and Freya's flight away from him, all the way back to the loss of his mother. He was preparing himself to meet a beast that might have come from nightmares, and he was not afraid.

Climbing down into the root system, he had the impression in places that the tree was more root than trunk. So much of the tree seemed to be root. The tree held up the world. And the roots held up the tree. And the roots themselves were not really buried in the earth.

They were not buried at all. So many of the roots had not found soil, so they twisted and writhed, like Rolf's own heart, and slunked about for water. There must have been a tap root, Rolf thought — the root that went straight down from the stem of the trunk and held the tree in place, within whatever rich soil there was down there beneath everything. He could not see it — all he could see was muck and moss and smoke — but he felt, even in his terrible mood, that it was there. Hidden like hope.

Rolf arrived in the mulch that went up to his thigh. And he waded through it into the gloom until he perceived the deeper darkness of a hole framed by petrifaction and stalagmites. He got the impression that something deep in the smoke of the hole was looking straight into his eye.

"*What are you doing here?*" asked the voice. "*What do you seek?*"

"Understanding," said Rolf, in a single word. Not "wisdom" or "knowledge," but "understanding." All his former fear was gone. Though, admittedly, there was a new fear that was creeping to the fore. A fear of the unknown that he now found himself facing, in all his new-found rage.

"*You do not want understanding,*" said the Dreki, with its own compulsive desire to call forth and boast the secrets of any visitor's heart. *"You want to be in your home. You want to be with your family. And now, by coming here, you have destroyed your family."*

"What do you mean?" asked Rolf, puzzled. His family had already been destroyed. Freya—

"You left your home," said the Dreki. *"You left in the middle of the night. You did not say goodbye. And yet it was the only place you loved. So betrayed did your sister feel—by your departure . . . so betrayed, after the adventures you two had shared—that she wept through the night and swept out of there in the morning."*

Rolf gasped. So Rat-A-Task really *had* lied to him. He really had. He had told Rolf his sister would leave him and so made it happen that Rolf left his sister. And why had he lied? So he could have a giant to carry him here, to this tree. He had lied to gain himself a bit of transportation.

The Dreki went on, still speaking of Freya.

"She combed the skies of Norway, Denmark, and Iceland, looking for where you might have ranged. But she did not find you. And so she cursed you. Cursed the giants and the world of men. She turned her back on all of it and took to the sky. Went to find the gods to let them convince her that they were her proper family. Your only home is she, and she hates you."

This was, to put it mildly, a lot to take in. And different from what Rat had said. Was it possible it was a whole different set of lies?

"Are you lying?" Rolf asked.

"Drekis never lie," said the Dreki.

"Except by omission," said Rolf, remembering what he'd heard the poet say.

"What could I possibly have left out?" asked the Dreki. *"Except perhaps a few choice curses that your sister might have thrown your way?"*

"But why are you telling me this?" asked Rolf. "I thought you wanted giants here."

"I do want giants here," said the Dreki. *"Just not you."*

"Why?"

"Because you cannot help me here. You would thwart my purposes."

"How?" asked Rolf.

"It is far too tiresome a thing to relate," said the Dreki. *"And you would not understand it."*

"Oh, I'm too stupid, am I?" asked Rolf. "I pledged to help the tree."

"That may be so, but you cannot help me."

"But how do you even know you don't want me?"

"Because I know."

And then the Dreki sighed a very big sigh.

"Very well," he said. *"I will tell you. You are not exactly what you seem to be. You look like a giant, but the pure blood of giants does not flow through your veins. You have mixed blood. This in itself is not so bad. It would be acceptable if the other portion of your blood were human."*

"My father is human," said Rolf. "Of course he's human."

"Ah, yes. But what about your mother?"

"What about her?"

"All your giant blood must have come from her. But was she a giant? Do you remember, as a baby, being cradled in the arms of a giant?"

Rolf was startled with the necessity of thinking again of his mother, something that upset him at the best of times. Here, surrounded by all this darkness, it was almost unbearable. Still, he remembered her eyes and her hair and her pale arms. He remembered his love for her. He remembered the doubt and disapproval in her eyes as she regarded him. How she laid him in the cradle and walked out of the room and then was gone forever. His eyes welled up with tears.

"No," he said. "She was not a giant."

"No, she was not," the Dreki continued. *"It would be acceptable if she had been part giant and part human. But it is clear she was more than that."*

"How?" asked Rolf. "How is it clear?"

"Is it not obvious? Look at your sister. Is she not special? Does she not speak the language of birds? Did she not sprout wings, leap from the ground, and soar up above the clouds? Did she not make you feel like a gargantuan clod on the flat, heavy earth?"

"Since you put it that way," said Rolf. "But what does that have to do with my mother and me?"

"Your sister," said the Dreki, *"proves that you are not entirely giant. You might be a big clumsy oaf with none of the attributes of your sister, but, like your mother before you, you must have some god in you. And that,"* he concluded, *"will not do at all."*

180

Rolf could not believe what he was hearing. Because he came from a family of humans and gods, because he had mixed blood, he would not be allowed to stay here, in the beautiful heart-stopping Tree of the World.

Still, he thought to himself, maybe it was time to leave anyway. The whole huge place reminded him of how he had failed his one little leaf.

But the sadness that overcame him at the thought of this was nothing compared to how he felt after what the Dreki said next.

"I already told all of this to that crafty little squirrel. I told him that I didn't want you. He said he needed you to get the rest of the giants, but that he would then send you home."

"He did not say that." Rolf could not believe his ears. Despite all the little selfish acts of the squirrel, this felt like too big a betrayal.

"He did," said the Dreki.

"He did not!"

"He did."

"HE DID NOT!"

And then Rolf heard the Dreki sigh.

"I'm so tired of arguing with small-minded creatures. You will leave here. I have seen it. It is inevitable. You will come to feel so dispirited by the little betrayals and false friendships that you will leave. It's very clear. There's no use even speaking about it."

Listening, Rolf's eyes welled up with tears. This creature, the Dreki, was right. He would leave here. He'd had quite enough.

"You're right," he said. "I don't know why I'm arguing with you." His voice started to break. "And do you know why you're right? I want to tell you. I don't even know why because you won't care, but at least you'll *know*, so I want to tell you. I loved a leaf."

It was hard to speak, he was crying so much, but he struggled to go on. "I did. I loved a little leaf. Her name was Idun. Egil the Poet killed her."

"Is that right?" asked the Dreki.

"Yes, that's right. I loved her. He killed her."

"It is true," said the Dreki. *"I'll confess, I care nothing for the fate of a tiny leaf. It is true too that I could not have predicted such a death, so small a thing it is in the grand scheme. A chess master does not heed the speck of dust that sits on the king's square. But I will say this: If Egil the Poet killed your leaf and this fact will drive you from your home in this tree, then everything is once again as it should be and all is right with the world."*

"Really?" asked Rolf, as he wept even more. "All is right with the world?"

"Yes," said the Dreki. *"All."*

Rolf stood for a moment, feeling anger and grief welling within him in equal measure.

"I am going to kill him," he said finally, not sounding like a child at all anymore. "I am going to kill Egil the Poet. And then you can have this tree all to yourselves again, you and your selfish little squirrel."

"Very good," said the Dreki. *"All is right with the world."*

"Although I really don't understand," said Rolf, "how a pair of creatures so unfeeling as the two of you could ever properly care for anything at all."

"It is not for you to understand," said the Dreki, almost cheerfully. *"So I would not worry about it if I were you. Run along."*

And then the smoke dissipated. The Dreki had withdrawn deeper into his petrified hole, leaving Rolf alone in the dark. He stood there in the muck for a long time. And then he began to make his way back, wondering whether little lives and little leaves and little loves always had to become intertwined with the supposedly great events being plotted by greater minds than his.

"If that is true," he thought to himself as he came to the trunk and began to climb, "then the world is a hateful place and I want no part of it."

18

The Giant Army

THE BEAKY was occupying himself by sewing a feathered coat of his own. He had (bravely, by any standard) made his way across the river below the waterfall, stepping and jumping from stone to stone. On the other side, before the tight copse of crow-dwelling trees, he had collected hundreds of discarded feathers. And then he'd made his way back (bravely again, especially considering he knew now how precarious it was) and winnowed the stash to produce only those feathers that proved to be most excellent and suitable to his purpose.

The Beaky had always kept a little sewing kit in the outer breast pocket of his coat, where the needle wasn't in danger of pricking him in some tender spot. It was something his mother had advised and he'd always remembered. The needle had been whittled from a bone he'd found once by the side of the road and kept against the occasion that he lost a button or tore a seam—particularly important in the former days when he had not wanted to stand out as being any different from his former fellow Bikki.

He had already spent several days on this feathered coat effort, trying to occupy himself so as not to worry about Egil the Poet and what he might be getting up to inside the cave at the top of the waterfall. Trying not to worry, either, about the enemies of Egil that might come. Trying not to worry about the Haralds. Trying not to worry about the giants. Most of all, he tried not to worry about the grumbling of his own stomach, which was empty nearly all the time after he'd run out of rations on the second day. On the fourth day he'd seen some dried sunflower stalks standing miraculously by the cliff and picked clean what had not already been eaten by the crows.

I should not be so grand as to call the thing he sewed a feathered coat. He never would have described it that way to anyone but himself. In truth it was more of a feathered ruff. He sewed a bunch of the shiny black feathers around the collar, enough for him to know he might feel them against his cheek from time to time. He knew he was never going to fly. Just to be clear. The Beaky may have been mildly deluded, but he was no idiot.

He was just taking a break from the task of reinforcing the threads three or four times over, sitting on an old log and wagging his throbbing fingers in the air, watching the crows at play in the copse across the river, when something in the distance caught his eye. He realized everything was about to get exciting again, a state he wasn't interested in at all.

The Haralds were coming back.

The Beaky went and untied the two horses and moved them deeper into the woods. Then he came back and climbed a small tree that was almost too fragile for his weight and bent down nearly to the ground. This suited him because he was a little afraid of heights. It was in a stand of trees some way away from the river, so he could observe the newcomers without being noticed by them.

And then, over the course of a half-day, he watched the Haralds come down the valley through the forest and into the clearing by the waterfall.

In the time they had spent apart from one another, the Haralds had all stopped being so many Haralds, despite the threat of some old witch, and started going by their own names again, behaving with their own personal styles.

One of them led the giants he brought in chains.

One of them led giants with beaming faces full of wonder at what was to come.

One of them walked side by side with the giants he

brought, sharing water and sights and stories and food. He had the biggest group, since the giants he walked with had found other giants along the way and convinced them to come. There were thirty of them.

One of them walked behind his group of giants, since he had lost the way and the giants knew the landscape very well. This was a big group too. Fourteen strong.

One of them came empty-handed, without any giants at all.

Most surprisingly (although perhaps not quite so surprisingly, when you think about it) was that the two actual daughters of Erik Blood-Axe came to the clearing by the river with their leather caps pulled off their heads and their hair hanging down. At least one of them did. The other had short hair, so it didn't exactly hang down, although her short hair was uncovered as well. And they came—these two—with giants that were girls: eight giants each, coincidentally, though one of the giants brought her little brother who was not a giant at all (though he hoped that he would prove to be a giant). His name was Fenn. And the names of the daughters of Erik were Astrid and Gudrun. The other sons, since we're on the subject, were Olaf and Tryggvi and Knut and Gull. The eldest, of course, was still Harald.

First thing that happened was that Gull—who was the second eldest brother and third eldest altogether, who had been the one to drag his assembly of giants to the river by force—received a thorough upbraiding from all his siblings as well as from many of the giants.

"I didn't know how to convince them," he protested as he removed the chains, arguing further that his skill in talking had gone by the wayside since he had thrown his lot behind his elder brother as one of the Haralds.

The other siblings quickly forgave him, though the giants did not. They all kept their distance from him. There were eighty of them, in all.

Harald, the eldest of the sons and daughters of Erik Blood-Axe, stood on the very outcrop that had served as The Beaky's sewing perch, and there he addressed the giants.

"Friends," he called. "I don't know how to address you, since you are giants. I always believed I would be your enemy, because, in the stories we have been told, giants are the enemies of the gods and therefore our enemies too.

"But I must tell you I am not your enemy today. I'm very happy to see you all. For two reasons.

"The first is that if there are so many of you here in our country, then perhaps there are gods hidden here too. You might not think that is such a good thing, but it's a good thing to me.

"The other reason is, we were asked to bring you here.

"Behind this cliff wall, there is a massive tree that stands so tall, it breaks through the blanket of clouds that covers our land and nearly touches the sun!

"It stretches down so low beneath us, into the ground, its very roots hold up the earth on which we stand.

"In other words, it is the Tree of the World—a place where it is always spring and summer, where the snow never falls like it has out here during this last year."

He paused for a moment. The Beaky, from his vantage point, could see the boy had made an impression. The young giants had all sat down to listen to him, even though the ground was wet and their bottoms would surely become damp. They seemed to have put all objections of mistreatment behind them, at least for the moment. That's how much they were already in thrall to his story.

"This place," Harald went on, "can be your new home. A place no one will ever be able to say is too small for you! You can climb all through the days with your fellows, up and down the boughs that are broad and sturdy enough to carry your weight, through bunches of leaves, catching sight of birds and beasts of every description. It will be a paradise for you. The tree itself welcomes you here. All it asks in return is that you serve as its protectors. What do you say?"

One of the eldest girl giants put up her hand. "We want to hear more of your story," she said.

"It's not just a story!" asserted Harald, betraying some impatience.

"Oh, we know that," said the giant. "But we want to hear more stories about it anyway. If you want to know the way to a giant's heart, you should know that our non-giant parents always stop telling us stories far too soon. As soon as we get big they think we have therefore become old! Too old to be told bedtime stories!"

"That's true!" agreed the boy named Fenn, who was her little brother. "They told stories to me but not to my sister!"

"Not to me either," said another giant.

"Nor me! Nor me!" shouted some others. All agreed wholeheartedly that Harald should tell them a few more stories before they ventured up the side of the cliff.

Harald, however, fancied himself someone who had certainly become too old for stories, and further, someone who considered words to be far less important than deeds. So he was about to reply that the time had come for these child giants to lay aside the memory of their thoughtless parents and grow up. Luckily, however, another giant spoke up before he could express the sentiment that would have turned them all against him.

"Tell us," asked another girl, "from whom are we to protect this tree?"

"I don't know," Harald confessed. "But I've seen it with my own two eyes, and I can tell you that when you see it for yourselves, you'll want to protect it as much as I do. You'll agree that pre-emptive steps should be taken—that *preventive* steps should be taken—to protect this tree from those who might come and cut it down. I know it might seem like a difficult thing to take preventive steps against an enemy we have no knowledge of.

But, the way I see it, a tree full of giants will have the effect of simply scaring people away, and that's pre-emptive and preventive enough for me.

"What's more," he continued, "when you see the tree, you'll know it's a very simple task we're asking of you, for you will know in your hearts that it is a small price to pay in exchange for the privilege to climb around inside something so beautiful!"

"That's well said, sir," answered the giant girl. "But what about him?"

"What about whom?" asked Harald, and then saw that her finger was pointing up and behind him toward the face of the cliff.

All the siblings (and The Beaky too) turned to see what the giants had already been watching for a little while. It was Egil. His back was to them, but he was clearly Egil. He was making his way swiftly like a spider, occasionally turning his head to look at them. Harald the eldest was about to say there was nothing to fear from this man, but something stopped him: a glint, in the poet's faraway eye, of white and blazing madness.

Had he not said that he might fight them when next they meet?

The Beaky himself, over at his new perch, could not believe the change that he perceived in the poet, even at this distance. Egil had seemed, in the brief time he'd known him, to be gnarled and hard and good, even if he always wanted to get his way and would not take no for an answer. But now his eyes were like split shells and his hair was twisted, stained with sap and standing straight up. His clothes were torn to rags and only the one foot was shod. The Beaky saw him leap the last few feet from the cliff to the ground, turn, and charge straight for the gathering.

Egil didn't know what was happening to him. He had been weeping silently and constantly since he'd pulled himself away from the bough and dragged himself up the tree, blind to everything he passed, even the enormous squirrel nest where the young giant sat deep in contemplation. He crawled up the tree, punching the trunk occasionally as he went, bruising and scraping his knuckles, until he finally arrived out on the ledge, where the spray of the water mingled with his bitter tears and he wondered what was supposed to become of him. He fell on his face on the rock and lay there for a long time. Afternoon passed and evening came, and then night and morning. Egil was so stupefied, he imagined himself again hanging upside down from the tree. It was difficult for him to understand everything that had happened, or how he had changed, or whether he had even changed at all. Time seemed to move backwards for him, and forwards again, and then backwards, like one of your modern horseless carriages, stuck in snow or mud.

At least until he peered over the edge of the cliff and saw the giants. The giants made him remember the

Dreki, and the Dreki made him remember his grief for his family, and the fact that the Dreki had killed his family. And the Dreki too had sent for all these giants. Egil had threatened to kill the giants. And now, he figured—well, why not?—he would kill the giants. It gave him purpose. It gave him something to do next, which is always important for a man who is full of rage and despair and who has nothing.

If he had stopped to think about it, even for a moment, instead of using his brain only as a second heart, pumping angry blood, Egil would have recalled that Idun the leaf, who had died to save him, would have stopped him from killing these giants with a single word.

And so, it must be added, would have his wife.

But this was as far as thought went in him. That is to say, not far at all. From here on in, it was all action.

Now he was on the ground at the foot of the cliff, and the giants were in front of him, sitting in the shallow snow by the riverbank. He began to run, forming a vowel in his throat. As he came, he spat it out and felt the Haralds fall before him. They were easy targets, the giants far more formidable. A sentence rumbled in his belly and worked itself up like bile into his lungs until he wanted nothing more than to cough it out and be rid of it like the pain of the world. He spat. He shouted. The faces of the giants were turned up toward him. Full of fear and wonder. They made him angry, but still he did not strike them. Words were far more violent and bitter to him, and they came out in vowels that seemed like so much nonsense. This was what it was to be a berserker. He spat and shouted and seethed and wailed until all his breath was spent and he fell to his knees, having vanquished, he thought, all his Dreki-bound enemies with paragraph after paragraph of words.

Then he heard someone speak. Someone near him. A young giant, looking down at him, even though the boy was sitting. His cheeks were red from blushing, but there was no fear in his eyes.

"Tell us another," said the boy.

Egil was out of breath. He did not understand. "Another what?" he asked.

"Another one of those," said the giant boy. "Another story, like the one you just told us."

"That was not a story," Egil wheezed, since he was almost too exhausted to speak.

"Then whatever it was," said the boy. "Perhaps it was a poem. Perhaps that is what a poem is. I've heard tell of poems, but I've barely even heard any stories in my life, so it's unlikely I would have ever heard a poem. Forgive me. Tell us another."

"That wasn't a poem!" Egil nearly shouted now that he had begun to catch his breath.

"What was it then?"

"It was DEFEAT!" shouted Egil. "It was RAGE! It was DESTRUCTION!"

"Then tell us another defeat!" replied the child, eagerly, happy to learn the correct words. "Tell us another rage. Tell us another destruction."

"You don't understand," said Egil, who was looking uneasily at them now, feeling the anger begin to ebb away in his exhaustion and even—was it possible?—his tears. "You don't understand."

"Then make us understand. Explain it to us."

Egil blinked a couple of times and looked up at them. They were all sitting on the ground. Even some of the Haralds were looking at him as if he were someone else. A wise person. Some of the others seemed as confused as Egil himself. He stared at them. They looked to him like they could be children. Like his own children.

"I am not your father, you know," he said, half indignant, blinking back tears, unsure of whom he was addressing. He felt a burble of rage inside him, felt it curl up in his stomach, as before, and seep up to fill his lungs. Soon he was going to shout again.

"Oh, I know that, sir," said the giant child. "Believe me. My father never said a word to me. Not since I grew big. He's never told me anything. Not like you at all."

The shout turned to water in his lungs and Egil coughed a couple of times and then began to sob. He sobbed for a good ten minutes, and everyone stood silently, not least The Beaky, over in his bent tree, who sat with his hand over his mouth and wept like a baby right along with him. The Beaky did not know why he was crying, did not know that this was the first time the man had ever wept in front of another human being, but he sensed how embarrassing it was for the poet, and even though he could not be seen, he averted his eyes and studied the toes of his boots, allowing the thought to creep into his mind that perhaps there was a way of affixing feathers there too.

In fact, they all sensed how embarrassing it was for the man to weep like this. All the former Haralds and the giants looked to the ground and respectfully waited for him to finish. He was silent for a long time and they all waited. They would have waited for days.

"One moment, one moment," Egil was saying, trying to find his way back to the dignity he already possessed.

(You may ask how he could be looking for something he already possessed. It's like when you spend ten minutes looking for your spectacles and then you realize you've been wearing them the whole time. Or your hat. Dignity is like that. Of course, the opposite is also true: You can think you have dignity when you actually don't, like when you think you're wearing pants when in fact you've forgotten to put them on and you walk out of your house in your underwear. It's been known to happen. I've done it myself now and again.)

"You must understand," Egil was saying. "You must understand . . . I lost my family—I lost my family—children, like you, who used to look up at me like that . . . and . . . used to ask, just like you, for me to tell . . . for me to tell them . . ."

"I'm sorry," said the child. And truly, Egil could see that he was. But he did not want him to be, for Egil was beginning to get a glimmer of what he was being given here. He'd been restored a vision of his family when they were living and happy, which was something that had never come to him in all the days and weeks and months since his tragedy had struck. The kind face of his wife had drifted over him, from time to time, but he had only ever been able to think of his children in the moment when they must have called his name and he had not come. Now he remembered them all, each of their smiling faces. And his old dog too. These giants held them in their expressions and the truth of it took Egil's breath away again and then it made him smile, and then sob again, and then look at the apologizing boy's face and laugh. He laughed so hard that it brought him to his feet and he clapped the giant boy on the shoulder.

"I give up!" he laughed. "You win!"

"We do?" asked the boy. "How do we win?"

"Just because!" And then he paused to work it out, and spoke more slowly. "Just because I hate a Dreki, and just because he called it correctly, doesn't mean I will murder a band of giant children. So the Dreki wins, and you win." And then he added. "And I win. And do you know what else?" he added.

"What else?" said the child.

"I am going to tell you all a whaling whopper of a story. That's what else," said Egil. "Just give me a minute to think it up."

But it turned out Egil was not quite finished with his fighting. Something glinted in the corner of his eye and he looked up.

19

Rolf the Ranger

THE EYES OF ALL assembled followed Egil's to the very top of the cliff. A figure had appeared at the lip of the ledge. His arms were in the air. Rolf. Clear as day it was him. The Haralds could see it and so could The Beaky.

Rolf the Ranger, for whom childhood had been left behind. If he'd been aware that his arrival was interrupting a whopper of a story, he would not have cared in the least. Why should other giants be allowed to hold onto their childhood, when he himself could not?

In a spectacularly unexpected move, Rolf leapt through the waterfall and dove straight down. It took several seconds for him to plunge into the river, where he skillfully flipped around and popped his head above the rushing water, swimming strongly toward the bank, as if he'd been doing it all his life. There appeared to be a little ball of fur clinging to his nose.

"Is this how everyone always arrives in this part of the world?" asked little Fenn to his sister.

"I don't think so," said the sister. "I think we just don't know the story."

"I hope someone tells it before too long," said Fenn.

"Me too," said the sister.

All the watchers had their mouths open as Rolf clambered up onto the side, pushed himself to his feet, and, without even stopping to shake himself off, charged, soaked and seething, straight for Egil, who was even now standing in the midst of the giants.

"I know you," the poet said. "We have a mutual friend. In fact, I've been asked to deliver a message . . ."

But Rolf wasn't listening. His two open hands collided with Egil's broad chest, sending him stumbling backwards.

"Why?" shouted Rolf.

"Why what?" asked Egil, a little shocked.

"Why are you just standing here *talking* to them as if you don't have a brutal plan?"

Then Rolf turned to the assembled giants.

"He's trying to trick you," he shouted, pointing an accusing finger at the poet. "Here he is talking to you. But really he wants to kill you. He's a liar and a trickster like everyone else. The world is full of them! Since you're all giants, you're probably gullible and naive, like me. You want to think the best of people. But I'm here to tell you that all the non-giant people—whether they be poets or Drekis or squirrels—are always going to try to get you to do things for them, usually by pretending to be your friend. But they're *not* your friend. This one here wants to kill you. But I won't let him!

"And I'll tell you," he added, wagging a finger in the face of Egil and the Haralds, though he was really still talking to the giants who, he felt, were just exactly like him. "There's a difference between being gullible and being stupid. Don't let *anyone* tell you you're stupid. You just want to be nice to people. You might think too that you're big clumsy oafs, because everyone always calls you that. But you just have to get used to your size. And when you do, then they'll be sorry. This one," here he pointed to Egil, "he'll be sorry too because he might be trying to fool you by making you all sit down so he can kill you, but he won't fool me! He's going to fight me right now!"

And then he turned to Egil, who was sitting calmly on the ground.

"Fight me!" Rolf cried. And then again, "Fight me!"

"No," said Egil, simply. And then, because he didn't want to upset the boy with the lightness of his reply, he spoke again more forcefully: "I won't!"

"You want to kill some giants!" shouted Rolf, undeterred. "So try it! Here's your chance! Fight me! Or are you a coward? Would you rather wait until I trust you? Until I think you're my friend? My sister," and here he turned again to address the crowd, "she had a friend. A good friend. A real friend. He was a falcon named Morton. They didn't even like each other at first, but they had so much in common that nothing could stop them from becoming friends. And he taught her things in a bird language they both spoke. He gave her everything, he gave her the wings off his back and they worked when she wore them! That's what I call friendship. That's what friendship is."

He turned back to Egil and asked him in a mocking tone, "Are you trying to be my friend? Can you do something like that for me?"

"No," said Egil. "I can't, but—"

"I didn't think so!" shouted Rolf. "Because only special people have special friends. My sister was special and I'm not! And I might as well just accept it! At least I know who I am! Even if I'm just an oaf, at least I know it! I'm not going to be gullible and I'm not going to ask anything from anyone! What do you think of that, mister poet? How are you going to manipulate me now? How are you going to manipulate any of us? Well, I'll tell you! You're going to fight me! And you're going to have to kill me, because otherwise I'm going to kill you."

"I don't know where you got the idea," said Egil, "that I want to kill giants, or that I'm going to fight you. I don't want to kill giants. I don't want to kill anybody."

"Don't cheat me with your words!" shouted Rolf, flinging angry tears. "Fight!"

"Cheat you? With my words? My boy, I would not

dream of it. My words are always fighting words, even when they're friendly."

"I don't care!" cried Rolf. "Don't give me words, you liar! Give me blows! And I will answer them, blow for blow, until one defeats the other, fair as war!"

"War is never fair," said Egil, starting to feel a little testy. He hated being called a liar, since it was likely he hated a liar as much as Rolf did. He went on. "Don't make me teach you to mind your manners."

"It's you whose mind should be mannered!" yelled Rolf, who did not even notice how he had misspoke.

The last thing Rolf wanted Egil to know was his true reason for wanting to fight. Egil had killed Idun the leaf. But Rolf felt no one could ever understand the value of the life of a leaf. If the Dreki could not, when a Dreki was supposed to be so smart, how could anyone? To Egil, Rolf thought, killing Idun would have been like stepping on the long grass and bending a blade, or breathing in a tiny insect with the air, or plucking a twig to pick at his teeth. Nothing to cry about. Especially nothing for a *man* to cry about, or any other creature for that matter, except a giant, who was vulnerable and loyal, perhaps because his heart was so big. But Rolf held a wound that had been inflicted deep inside his heart with the knowledge of Idun's murder, and it was his own enduring wish that it be kept hidden and never be revealed, lest his enemies laugh at him. Egil would have victory over him, Rolf believed, only if the truth of his anger was revealed. So he kept shouting and kept fighting and kept pushing away any thought about why it was that he wished to fight.

Rat-A-Task was there too, however. He still clung to Rolf's nose, biting it. He scurried up over the crown of Rolf's head to bite first one ear and then the other. Perhaps he'd been a little vehement, always trying to get what he wanted. But that didn't make him a bad squirrel (did it?). His mother had told him, you should always try to get what you want, and that if you stepped on a few toes, it didn't matter because you were only just a squirrel and stepping on a few toes wouldn't hurt.

And just because he'd lied to Rolf (sort of), did that really mean he was not his friend? They'd spent all this time together. The giant boy had helped him get to the tree and build his nest. Sure, he had not exactly told the truth about the boy's sister, but it might have been the truth. Nobody really knew what she was going to do. And did it really matter, in the end, who left home first? All children leave their homes eventually. All his own brothers and sisters, for example. They'd all left before he did. Even his mother left before he did.

Rat-A-Task wanted to explain all this to Rolf, but there was a much more pressing matter, which was that he did not want Rolf to kill the man anymore. From the ledge atop the cliff he had seen—as Rolf had too—all the giants make peace with Egil the Poet. Everything, as far as Rat-A-Task was concerned, was going swimmingly. So he did not understand why Rolf would still wish to attack this man. He worried that such an attack would turn the man against them all again, so that he would lay waste to all the squirrel's best laid plans. There is an expression: The best laid plans of mice and men. But a squirrel's plans are the best laid plans of all.

So Rat had to stop Rolf somehow.

At first, he thought he might come up with something like, *Don't attack the man! His fingers are as sharp as knives! He'll slit your throat before you even have a chance to land a blow!* But all evidence suggested that Rolf wasn't going to believe a lie like that. Oh well. A glorious era, wherein a tiny squirrel could control the mind of an enormous giant, had come to an end. Rat had to cut his losses and bring this giant boy's anger to a stop. He had to tell him the one true thing he'd held back all this time: that the Dreki did not want him here; that no one wanted him here. That it was time for Rolf to leave. To go home. Even if there was no home to go to, even if all that had been taken away. Still, Rolf had to go there.

So the squirrel took a deep breath and scurried down inside Rolf's shirt, around the collar to the back, preparing for the leap up to Rolf's ear, thinking hard about how to choose the words. Thinking so hard, in fact, it made his little squirrel head hurt.

Meanwhile, back in the world outside the vicinity of a giant's ear, Rolf had managed to work Egil up into a fighting mood. The onlookers held their breath, without any idea what these two might do. They did not really believe this man could hurt anyone. Perhaps the pair would soon bring this story to an end and then take a bow together.

But it did not seem to be going that way.

"I'm going to teach you a lesson," said Egil to Rolf. "Not to speak to your elders like that."

The bad-tempered poet drew his dagger, since the scabbard that would have held his sword was empty. Rolf, for his part, leapt across the river in a single bound and lumbered over to a small stand of trees, yanking one out by the roots and sending a party of shrieking crows up into the snowy air. If anything was proof that anger had gripped the giant, this was it. Rolf had once sworn he would never harm a tree again.

The boy giant charged again toward Egil, leaping back over the water and swinging his weapon in circles over his head. It was almost too big for him, nearly knocking him off his feet.

Egil, for his part, leapt and rolled out of the tree-swinging giant's path. But then, as he stood, he slipped on the wet ground and then tripped on an exposed root, falling flat on his face in the mud and snow. When he rolled over and looked up into the cloud cover of Norway, he saw that young Rolf was standing over him, taking up almost every part of Egil's field of vision and wielding his dying tree. The poet realized he was not going to be able to roll out of the way.

"I only just felt like starting to live," he muttered. "How funny is that?"

The sky above Rolf looked suddenly so beautiful to

Egil, clouds like mountains rolling into the distance. A light breeze played with the giant's hair. Far overhead, a raven circled lazily. Egil's vision was so clear in fact, he could see patterns in the bark of the trunk about to come down on his head. He even thought he saw a small red squirrel leap from the inside of the giant's collar and hang swinging from the lobe of an ear.

And then a change came over Rolf. The boy giant stopped, as all the rage bled out of his face. He stumbled back a few paces and then placed the tree gently down onto the ground beside him. Then he reached up around his head and, gently, pulled a little squirrel out from the hair behind his right ear. Like he was performing a magic trick for Egil's benefit.

So the squirrel really had been there; Egil's eyes had not tricked him. The poet could see too, again, that this giant was still a little boy, despite all the effort taken to work himself into a murderous rage. It was a good thing, thought Egil, for a boy to be a boy. Though it must have been hard at the moment.

What the poet did not yet realize was just how this very much felt like the end of the line for Rolf the Ranger.

The giant boy stumbled back a bit more, then crouched down on his haunches, allowing the squirrel to scurry up onto his open palm and sit there. Then the giant spoke in a sad, vulnerable voice:

"What did you say?" he asked.

"Chitter chitter chitter chitter," replied the squirrel, somewhat too vehemently, Egil thought, considering how softly the giant had spoken. Still, despite the tone, this chittering sounded to the poet pretty much like nothing at all.

He knew it was not nothing though.

"You . . . ," said Rolf, and then paused for a moment before taking the thought up again. "You want me to go home?"

"Chitter chitter chitter," replied the squirrel.

"This is my punishment?" asked the boy, and there was a real wounded sound in his voice now. "For attacking the man? My punishment? To go home?"

And then, through the squirrel's further chittering, Egil saw the boy giant think and think and grow sadder, and hesitate to speak and then speak nonetheless. "You know," the boy said, "you don't have to lie to me. You don't have to make it sound like a punishment for something I did that was wrong. You could just tell me that the Dreki said I had to go home. I know that already."

Egil almost wept to hear these words. In the sound of the child's voice he distinctly heard the last little bit of a heart breaking.

"You could just be straight with me," Rolf went on. "I know it's in your nature to lie but, I mean, did you not hear anything I just said? You could just . . . tell me the truth. It would have been the same. I would have had to leave no matter what. But at least I would have known you had a little bit of respect for me."

He was sniffling a bit. "Because I still helped you.

I still protected you. I still carried you through the forest and climbed the side of the cliff and got you into the tree. I still helped you build your winter drey. I know you were lying to get me to help you, but I still helped you and that should be worth something. I thought it would mean you might have a little more trouble telling me I had to go away."

Involuntarily, he let out a little sob. But he did not want to cry and so he swallowed it. And went on again.

"I mean, if you're going to lie to me anyway, then why don't you do it to say something nice? Why can't you use it to say I can stay? Like, for just a little bit longer? Why do you have to make it hurt so much? What difference does it make, really, whether I stay inside a tree that's as big and bigger than the whole world? I know I'm not worthy. I know I have mixed blood and so I'm not really fully a giant, and so that means I can't. I heard that already. So . . . but . . . why can't you tell me *nice* lies? Why do you have to hurt me?"

"Chitter chitter chitter," said the squirrel.

"I was going to hurt that man," said Rolf. "I see. But do you even have any idea how he already hurt me? How he already hurt someone who was *dear* to me? Would you even care if I told you? Oh . . ." He sighed the sigh of an old man. "What does it matter? What difference does it make? I don't want to stay in that tree anyway. It will just remind me . . ."

He choked up and then calmed and started again. "It will just remind me how I had a friend. How I had sworn to protect my friend. But I didn't. And so maybe that makes me a liar too. Why should I even judge you for being a liar when I'm a liar too?"

Now Rolf put his head down and cried for a bit and everyone waited for him to continue. Finally he raised his head and spoke again.

"I loved a little leaf," he said. "Laugh if you like. I don't care anymore. Yes, I loved a leaf and I swore to protect her. But I failed. So maybe I deserve to be banished from this place. Maybe it's good for a giant to remain clumsy and gullible. Maybe when a giant stops being gullible, when he learns about lies, maybe that's when he becomes a murderous, dangerous creature, a betrayer of little loving leaves and a liar to boot. And then how could he deserve to stay in such a beautiful place?"

Here he turned and spoke briefly to the giants. "Because it *is* a beautiful place," he said. "You're going to love it there. And you should forget everything I told you before and stay naive and gullible and never make friends with a giant like me because I'll just teach you how to lie and how to be mistrustful and how to be disappointed with the world."

Rolf turned back to address the squirrel in his palm. He was unsteady for a moment, like he might fall over, but he went on.

"I thought these giants would be my friends. I thought we would all live together in your beautiful winter drey. But it doesn't matter. I don't know them yet anyway. They're all still strangers to me. Even if I did . . . even if I did get to know them, I would probably let them down. Just like I did to Idun!"

And then Rolf finally started to weep and weep. The giants had all moved in closer, since he was speaking very quietly to the squirrel in his palm, and they wanted to hear every word. Egil, for his part, wanted to move a little further away, since he was still lying at the giant's feet. But he didn't want to distract the boy from what he was saying. He felt the words that came out of this giant were fragile, like soap bubbles or a balancing act in a travelling minstrel show. Such words were like poetry, even if they were misguided. Poetry is about telling the truth of the heart, and Egil did not wish to disturb the boy from his speaking.

"Chitter chitter chitter," said the squirrel, and Egil thought the words might be as meaningless as he understood them to be. Still, he had to admit he would have given his eye teeth to understand what the little creature was saying.

"I know she was a leaf!" Rolf replied, raising his voice just a little. "I know! And I know too that the idea of a friend isn't important to you. You're just so singular. I know the Dreki would never think to spare the life of a leaf. He's too busy thinking about the bigger story. The story of everything. But it's true that I was friends with this leaf, I really was. And her name was Idun. She spoke to me and she was a good and loving and noble friend. She was *my* friend!"

Rolf put his head down again and wept quietly, not caring anymore at all what anyone thought about anything.

And then a voice spoke up, saying the most surprising thing.

"She spoke to me too."

It took Rolf a few seconds to figure out where this had come from.

The man on the ground in front of him.

"I beg your pardon?" said the giant, since his first instinct was always to be polite and also because he could speak more than single words now as a matter of course and also because he could not believe his ears.

"She spoke to me too," said Egil. "Though I would never say she was the friend to me that she was to you. I am sure of one thing, however, and that is that I owe her my life. So I honour your friendship with her. And I will defend your friendship and fight anyone who laughs at you. Because I know."

"You?" said Rolf, since he still could not believe his ears.

"Yes," said Egil. "Me."

"But you killed her," said Rolf simply.

And all the giants gasped as one and looked to the poet on the ground. Accusingly.

"No," said Egil. "I did not. Or at least I did not mean to. She worked to save my life, and by her work she grew old, and by growing old she died. And I'm so sorry for your loss. She fell like a leaf in the fall. But she did not die before saying goodbye and she did not die before passing on her greeting and her love and respect and farewell to you, Rolf the Ranger. In the nine days that I knew her, you were the only creature she ever spoke of. She loved you, and she was your friend too. It did not just go one way."

Rolf was speechless. "She saved you?"

"I was hanging upside down," explained the poet. "Trapped in a snare for nine days. She worked for all those nine days, every minute of them, to save my life. Without her efforts, she would be alive and I would be dead. I suspect that would be a better arrangement for the world, but there's nothing I can do about it."

"Then," said Rolf, quiet and hard, "it was I who killed her, and not you at all."

"No," said Egil. "How could you have? You weren't even there."

"Because it was I who trapped you in that snare. I trapped you in that snare and was too scared to come and set you free."

"You set that snare?" Egil asked. "But why?"

And then, all at once, he realized.

"You overheard me," he said. "You came here thinking I was going to kill all these giants because you overheard me talking to the Dreki."

Rolf nodded.

"I understand," said Egil. "I must have sounded very scary to you. But that was just my bluster. And that unpleasant, all-seeing Dreki knew it too. I don't suppose you overheard the part where he told me he knew I could never kill innocent creatures?"

Rolf shook his head.

"Well, it serves me right," said Egil, "because I should know better than to speak words that aren't true. But again, that was my fault, not yours. That was my bluster and you believed me and acted to protect your fellow giants and your tree. Those were my lies, and I suffered by them. And so did you."

"And Idun died for it," Rolf mumbled, his head hanging down.

"That's right," said Egil. "Idun died for it."

Rolf nodded and tried to hold his composure, but he could not. He cried out now like a wolf drifting alone on an ice floe in the middle of the North Sea. The unfairness of his whole life was suddenly right there, inside him.

"But I didn't even see her grow!" he said at last. "I hardly even got to know her!"

And then he spoke to Egil again. "And she died helping you, just like Morton died helping Freya. Such gifts these creatures have to give! I don't even know what that's like! Freya's gone and Morton's gone and my father's gone and my mother's gone and this little squirrel in my hand—he trusts me not to hurt him, but that isn't the same as to say he's my friend. He isn't my friend. He just needed my help for something. And he got it. And now even little Idun is gone. One little leaf among millions, and so why should I care? But I care! And who will help me?"

Rolf looked up at the cloudy sky and the tears were streaming down his face. "Who will help me?"

"I'll help you," said Egil, still on the ground. "You can bet on it. I'll help you."

And then the poet raised his voice for all to hear. And there was an edge of command in it. "For starters, no one, whether he be a big bad Dreki or a chittering little squirrel, is going to stop my friend, Rolf the Ranger, from living in this tree with all his friends. Because he has a lot of friends. I'm his friend, and I suspect he's made a lot of other friends today."

Egil swept both hands over the assembled giants. "Are you not his friends?" he asked.

"Yes!" they cried as one, in a voice that was louder than anything Rolf had ever heard, even in the clash and din of battle. "Yes!" they shouted again. "We are his friends!"

"And you?" Egil now addressed the Haralds. "Are you not his friends?"

The sons and daughters of Erik Blood-Axe had been unable to help themselves and were moved beyond measure by what they had witnessed.

"We are," they said. And the eldest spoke further. "Nothing bad, it seems, can come from a heart so big as the one that beats in this giant's chest. For myself, I would be honoured to call him my friend and fellow protector of the Tree of the World."

"And you?" Egil now turned toward The Beaky, who had witnessed everything and had believed all this time that he had not been seen. "Are you his friend?"

The Beaky, it must be said, could hardly speak, so grateful was he to be living in a time of such spirit, even with all the uncertainty in the world. He, a former henchman, and a cowardly one at that, had been allowed to witness the great stirrings of history.

"I don't think it really matters," said The Beaky, "whether this noble young boy has a friend in poor, poor Bikki Number Four."

"It matters," said Egil.

"Well, I am his friend, in any case," said The Beaky. "And fellow defender even. Though I'm not sure I'll have the nerve to get up into that tree."

"I can help you with that," said Egil. And here he raised his voice again, presumably for the benefit of the little squirrel who had quietly slunk back into Rolf's collar. "Because friends don't banish friends from trees. Especially this tree. This Tree of the World."

20

Home

EGIL DID NOT REALLY believe in the Tree of the World, despite what he said. For sure, he had entertained some notions as he descended into its depths, and then too while he was hanging delirious and dying, upside down from its branches. But he never believed it could really be much more than a particularly large tree that happened to grow in a particularly large shaft behind a particularly high cliff. Stranger things had happened. Stranger things, in fact, had happened to him. So no one would ever stir up any faith in him by telling him how rare it was, this tree that had grown and these things that had happened.

Still, it was a beautiful place to come to, and a good place to settle down, at least if he didn't spend too much time contemplating the invisible and (he felt) malign intelligence that dwelled down there in its depths. And now, as he led the giants up the side of the cliff and into the tree, he felt that he would have to make do, for the moment, with all these contradictions. A safe place that had a dangerous dweller beneath. A beautiful place that had a hidden ugliness, or at least a hidden thing that would not show its face.

Egil cajoled The Beaky into overcoming his fear of heights, telling him there was no greater reward for mastering such fear than to see the spectacular tree. And so The Beaky had bid farewell to his good horse Nicker, and then he climbed and cried and cried and climbed. And he was a good climber too. Eventually he came to the top and crawled through the crevice. He was awed by what he saw there, to put it mildly, and opted to stay and squire himself to Egil.

All the giants, of course, pledged to stand by Rolf—as if they were all sisters and brothers together and Rolf one of them. The squirrel had chittered and chattered and seemed to complain, but there was really nothing he could do. They had all declared, in no uncertain terms, that if Rolf left, they would all leave and there would be no one left at all to protect the tree.

For his part, Rat-A-Task crossed his paws and hoped that everything had somehow taken place according to the Dreki's master plan, and that he was not after all breaking any rules. And he resolved to visit the Dreki at his earliest convenience, as soon as he worked up the nerve, and give him a report as to what had taken place there, in the belowland by the river. Perhaps, Rat-A-Task felt, the Dreki would finally give him some words—a message—to take up the tree and say to those who might be perched in its utmost branches. An imperious hawk, perhaps, with golden wings, who would turn his head and regard the squirrel with a cold and ancient eye, up there in the crown: The part where the branches grow higher when the trunk has come to its highest point.

The Haralds climbed as well up and into the tree. They learned how to swing around within its branches like monkeys, since they were all so much smaller than the giants, serving to remind anyone who might have forgotten that they were just children too. How they longed to play at games that were not always war.

Still, after many days and weeks living with their new friends in the tree, the Haralds recalled their pledge to search for the hidden gods of Norway. And so they returned to behaving like boys and calling themselves boys, and calling themselves Harald, after their grandfather, Harald Finehair, uniter of Norway. And they said goodbye to their friends and climbed down out of the tree and marched away, as a single group, to find their gods and introduce themselves.

And Rolf. You should have seen him. He learned how to smile. Which was really something to see. After some months and years, he even learned how to laugh, which, in this bitter world, is as heroic an act as anything.

He had a family now, a school of giants the way you might call a group of fish a school, only these were giants. They were there to play with and talk to and work together and climb up and down and around and across, through the many embracing arms of this tree. Together they helped the squirrel to build the most massive winter drey that had ever been built.

And Egil helped them too. He had nothing better to do. He was a surrogate father now, to this bunch, or at least to Rolf and that was enough. But really to all these giants. Who demanded, night after night, their beloved bedtime stories, before drifting off to sleep in their child giant clumps. Egil told so many, he began to think he might write them down in a saga. And that meant laying aside his grief and his anger and his warring words and ways. That meant coming to believe in this Tree of the World, despite the fact that he was not a great believer in anything.

As his beard grew long and his hair grew white, Egil sometimes wondered why the Dreki had wanted Rolf banished, why it had tried so hard to drive Egil himself away. Surrogate father and surrogate son, then, had something in common. Egil and Rolf. And that was itself enough to bind the one to the other, at least in Egil's mind. He sometimes wished he could divine the Dreki's mysterious vision of the future. But it did not seem to matter. The future, in point of fact, does not exist. No matter what some old Dreki says. And in fact, the Dreki remained so silent, during all the time that passed, down there in the depths below the crust of the earth, that Egil all but forgot about him. Everyone did. Well, almost everyone. They were too busy building a home together inside the Tree of the World, with its sunny spring and summer days within the funnel of a cloudless sky.

This was the story of how a lonely boy came to make many friends, and to live in a good place, simply by helping a little squirrel who did not even deserve his trust. How he came to see many things. How the wound of the loss of his sister came to be salved. How he grew to become a man-giant, six times his former size, though still not too big for the Tree of the World, which itself kept growing until it came to be of massive, almost planetary size. How time moved through the tree both swiftly and slowly. How he was happy there. How he never forgot the little leaf Idun and the lessons she taught him: How something so small could make a difference in someone's life, could come to be so important that it might even stop a life from ending too soon. Or even a world. Could even stop a world from ending too soon.

Acknowledgements

Thanks to Romeo Thomas Walters, Athanasia Sophia Walters, Marianne Apostolides, Katerina Cizek, and Jane Wells for being readers. Thanks to Kent Dixon for giving me the idea.